The Baby Arrangement

Tara Taylor Quinn

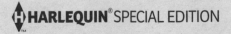

HARLEQUIN® SPECIAL EDITION

Recycling programs
for this product may
not exist in your area.

ISBN-13: 978-1-335-57372-8

The Baby Arrangement

Printed in U.S.A.

Having written over eighty-five novels, **Tara Taylor Quinn** is a *USA TODAY* bestselling author with more than seven million copies sold. She is known for delivering intense, emotional fiction. Tara is a past president of Romance Writers of America and is a seven-time RWA RITA® Award finalist. She has also appeared on TV across the country, including *CBS Sunday Morning*. She supports the National Domestic Violence Hotline. If you need help, please contact 1-800-799-7233.

Visit the Author Profile page
at Harlequin.com for more titles.

For Finley Joseph.
May you always be aware how very much
you were wanted.
You've filled holes in many hearts, Little Man.

Chapter One

She didn't want dinner. She wanted his support of her plan to buy herself some sperm.

Excited in a way she hadn't been in far too long, Mallory Harris calmed herself as she waited for Braden to join her at the upscale, quiet restaurant he'd chosen for the meeting he'd called. Staring out the wall of windows toward the harbor, watching people walking along the decks of a cruise ship that had docked, she turned her attention to the pink skies beyond, the miraculous beauty of the sun's final rays gracing the Pacific before it would drop beyond the horizon for another day.

Wishing she'd ordered a glass of wine, she changed her mind and did so. A glass of her favorite California-grown Sauvignon Blanc. Braden would be expecting her to have one and she didn't want any raised eyebrows until she was ready to deliver her spiel.

A little liquid courage didn't hurt, either, though she wasn't normally one to seek sustenance from anyplace except inside herself. And somewhat from Braden. She and her ex-husband might not be simpatico, but she still trusted his judgment on most things. Things that didn't deal with actual emotions.

He'd had a reason for the upcoming dinner. Though they ate out together on a fairly regular basis, it was never just to eat. There was always something to talk about requiring them to come together.

Speculating about the reason for the meeting was wasted energy, she'd decided long ago. After three years of being post-divorce friends, she and Braden had found a groove with which they were both relatively comfortable. At least she thought so.

One was never quite sure how Braden felt—probably not even him. If ever a man was disconnected from his emotional side, it was Braden.

All water under the bridge. Not her problem anymore.

He was probably going to tell her he was seeing someone. Why he felt the need to confess to her every time he saw a woman more than once was beyond her. They were divorced. Technically, she no longer had a right to know.

Or even a desire to know.

Her wine arrived and she took a sip. Okay, maybe a little piece of her, way deep inside, liked that he told her about his relationships. Like she was in one step deeper than the women he told her about. Shaking her head, she pushed the thought away—as far as she could get it.

Wanting to be inside Braden's deep places wasn't healthy. She'd very purposely and specifically chosen, through much personal work and counseling, to get herself outside of him. To stay outside of him. Lest she waste her life in a vortex of void and unfulfilled need.

Or feel like she had to hide every time she had a tear to shed. Being ashamed of her grief was something she'd worked long and hard to get past.

Braden had never meant her to feel shame, she knew that. But when someone got uptight every time you cried, or, worse, walked out when you cried, you ended up with learned reactions that weren't necessarily accurate. Humiliation. Mortification. Guilt. And a host of other words she'd heard bandied about during her group grief sessions.

So yeah, wine was good. If he thought her idea was nuts, she wasn't going to cry. Or even be embarrassed. She was going to remind herself that they were divorced and that she had every right to pursue single parenthood. That, for some women, it was not only the best choice, but the only real workable choice.

When the waitress came by again, she ordered a beer for Braden. She'd purposely arrived early enough to not risk walking in with him—looking or feeling like a couple. When they were meeting others, it didn't bother her to travel together, but when it was just the two of them, she had her rules. Her boundaries.

They never spoke of them, but he respected them just the same. She always got there at least fifteen minutes early. He'd arrive exactly five minutes before the designated time.

Unless he texted to say he was going to be late.

Or she did.

They had the friendship down to a science.

Now if only she could be certain that he was going to be friendly about the new direction her life was about to take. With all of the preliminary testing and physical exams done, the paperwork filled out and money paid, all that was left before the actual procedure was letting him know. She could do it without him. Would do it without him.

But life was still better with Braden in it.

She'd changed after work. It wasn't a big deal for her to have done so. Her house was only a couple of miles from the daycare—and from the harbor restaurant he'd chosen for dinner. Braden just noticed, as he was walking across the room to meet her, that she looked phenomenal in black leggings and that tight-fitting cream-colored shirt. He'd been expecting jeans and a Bouncing Ball polo shirt. After all, she didn't know that this meeting was major, as opposed to the more general passing of news for which they normally came together.

She didn't need to know that the sight of her still turned him on.

Working in the same high-rise executive office building as they did, albeit with his property management and real estate business taking up the top floor and her daycare housed in a double suite on the ground, they could chat there any day they chose. They just, by some unspoken agreement, didn't choose to.

No point in having people who shared their professional days gossiping any more than necessary about the couple who'd divorced after their five-month-old baby died.

The pity, even after all this time, was hard to take. He had no desire to feed the trough.

He was hungry, though, and ready, as he slid into the booth across from his ex-wife, to order a big juicy steak. She'd have some kind of meal-sized salad.

He'd never been a salad kind of guy.

Taking a long sip of the beer she'd ordered for him, he smiled at her, liking the warm gaze she sent back in his direction. Maybe he was making a mistake, transferring himself a little further out of her life, but he had to do something or they were both going to stagnate and die.

By the end of their smile, the waitress was standing there, tablet in hand ready to take their order. Without looking at the menu, they both told her what they wanted. She thanked them, took their menus, turned around and he all but pushed her away from the table.

He had to get this over with. Plans for his move to L.A. were moving rapidly. He needed Mallory to know.

And to fully understand, from the outset, that he wasn't selling the building in San Diego or in any way changing their business arrangement. It had been in effect before they were married and would remain for as long as she wanted The Bouncing Ball, her highly successful daycare, to be housed in the executive office building that used to be his only commercial holding but was now one of many.

He raised his beer to her glass of wine and sipped it, words spilling in his head, unable to utter them. Not at all like he'd decided this would go.

He knew he just had to say what he'd come to say. That he was acquiring land north of L.A. to build a professional complex similar to the one they now shared in San Diego, and he would be moving there for the foreseeable future.

"I'm going to have a baby."

Good thing his beer was close to the table. When it slipped out of his hand, it didn't break. And barely spilled.

Mouth hanging open, he sat there, too dumbfounded to say anything.

"I just wanted you to know."

He stared. White noise from the room around them faded.

"I'd kind of hoped you'd be supportive, but if you'd rather not know about it, hear about it, I completely understand."

He didn't move.

She did. Standing, she touched his arm. "I'm so sorry, Bray. I had no idea the news would upset you so much. I guess… I mean, in light of the fact that the last time we did it together… I mean…with losing Tucker… I should have been more sensitive. I just… I'm the one who's been dragging us both down with my inability to move on and I'm really excited about this. I just… couldn't wait to let you know that I…"

Her fingers on his arm were nice. Familiar. Tender and light.

"Sit." He got the word out, then followed it with, "Please."

He took a full breath when she quickly slid back into her seat.

"I'm sorry," he said. He'd broken an understood rule— one was never to make the other unduly uncomfortable or bring an overabundance of emotion into their joint atmosphere.

He could blame it on her for laying something like that on him, but they were allowed to tell each other anything they wanted to share. That had actually been a spoken agreement. Reiterated more than once, by both of them, in the early days of their post-divorce relationship.

Hell, for all he remembered they'd said it to each other like a vow during the actual divorce proceedings. They'd said several things meant for their ears only when they'd sat before the judge that day, holding hands.

He shook his head and sipped his beer.

"You're pregnant." He got the words out and he wasn't cut as sharply by the sound as he'd expected. Who in the hell had gotten his ex-wife pregnant?

The unwelcome words kept repeating, like an annoyingly bad rhythm, in his mind. He wouldn't speak them. They weren't cool.

"Not yet." From the crease in her brow, the way she leaned toward him slightly, the hint of an upward curve on those beautiful lips, he knew she was placating him. Dammit.

And yet…she wasn't pregnant?

Holy damn. Relief eased the sweat that had popped up all over his suited body.

"But you've met someone."

The truth still loomed. She was going to have another man's baby. Start a family separate and apart from him.

The implication he was to draw from that followed almost immediately.

She was moving on.

This was good news.

Very good news.

Exactly-what-he-wanted news.

But he wasn't smiling anymore.

Mallory had someone else to watch her back now. She was finally over the past enough to start anew.

He was free.

Chapter Two

Braden was going to give himself a crick in the neck if he didn't quit the exaggerated nodding.

Prior to that, he'd sipped his beer a couple of times and some expressions had flitted across his face. She wasn't going to put herself back into near suicidal mode by trying to decipher them. Or make more of the hint of despair than was meant to be there.

Braden didn't allow himself to acknowledge despair, nor was he all that comfortable around those who did. For all she knew, he honestly didn't get the feeling. Not like she did.

He'd gotten the love, though, hadn't he? Back before Tucker died. No one could deny, seeing him with their son, that he'd adored that boy.

Tears stung her eyes while welling emotion clogged her throat. She took a sip of wine, forcing her muscles to relax. She was not going to do this. She would not fall prey to feelings of inadequacy around her ex-husband—which meant she couldn't cry in front of him.

It had been an unspoken rule between them since they'd decided to stay friends after the divorce.

And the best way to not burst into tears was to think happy thoughts.

He was wearing one of her favorite Braden ensembles. Dark grey suit with just a hint of lighter threading, the striped shirt in grey, black and white with the maroon tie. At six-two, with that lush, thick, dark hair and those baby blue eyes, Braden could easily have been voted sexiest man alive.

"No, I haven't met someone," she said after the silence between them had stretched a bit too long. "I'd have told you if I had. You know that."

There were some things they counted on from each other. Telling him if she was moving on was one of them.

Which was probably why he was always informing her when he was seeing someone. He hadn't ever seemed to get to the point of seriously moving on, though. He dated, he fizzled, he dated, he fizzled.

His frown brought back a wave of tension. "I don't understand, then."

"I'm going to be artificially inseminated," she told him. And then, before he could voice an opinion of any kind, she barged full force ahead with the spiel she'd practiced in bed the night before and in the car on the way over, too.

"With the advance in research and technology, and with changing lifestyles, more women than ever are using sperm banks to have children. There's even an acronym for us, SMC, Single Moms by Choice," she said—not at all what she'd practiced. "I've already had all of the exams and testing done. I'm using a facility in Marie Cove, forty-five minutes south of LA. They're fertility specialists, not a sperm bank. I met with the owner when I was looking at places and I just really like her. I got a good feeling when I was there.

"It could take up to six tries, and I'm prepared for that, financially and emotionally," she continued, speaking to the man she knew him to be—one who dealt with facts, with reality, and shied away from the emotional aspects of being alive.

She didn't blame him. She'd met his mother and his sister many times. She had sat next to him through countless phone calls where they'd tried to get him to side with them against whoever they felt had slighted them, from something as menial as someone using a hurtful tone of voice against one or the other of them, or their claim that someone had been deliberately manipulative or demeaning. As the only male influence in their home growing up, he'd spent his youth learning how to bypass the drama to get to the truth of whatever might need attention.

"Way back in the '80s, more than 30,000 children were born as a result of donors," she told him. "There hasn't been any numerical research collated since then as there's no one body of collation, no database. But judging by the sheer volume of clinics today and the number of clients they have, you can logically guesstimate that the number of births has risen well into the hundreds of thousands."

She'd gotten out of bed the night before, in the middle of preparing her spiel, to do that particular research. For him. She really wanted him to be okay with her choice.

He was still sipping beer. Watching her.

"I'm going to do this, whether you approve or not,"

she told him. "I'd love your support. It means a lot to me." She paused, sipped her wine and hoped dinner didn't come for a while because her stomach was in knots. "It means a whole lot to me," she added. "But my decision is made."

Because she'd had to be certain that she was doing the right thing for her life. She hadn't even told Tamara yet. But she was fairly certain her friend from grief counseling would approve. Though Braden hardly knew the woman who'd lost four babies—three to early term miscarriages and one a viable birth but too premature to sustain life—Mallory felt as though she and the other woman were soul mates in a lot of ways.

His expression gave away very little. He was studying her.

Was he trying to figure out how to diffuse this emotionally wracked tangent she was on?

She watched him back, knowing her last thought wasn't fair. Not to either of them. Braden had always shown her the utmost respect when it came to her life choices. And he had often times sought her advice when it came to his own matters. Still did.

Their waitress stopped to say their dinners were almost ready and asked if he'd like another beer. He nodded. Her wine glass was still more than half full.

"Say something," she told him when the waitress walked away.

"There's a light in your eyes I haven't seen in…well, too long."

She smiled. "I've found my future," she told him softly.

Then he shook his head. And she braced herself. She wanted his support, so she had to listen to his concerns.

It wasn't like there weren't any. She had them, too. She readied her answers as their waitress delivered his beer.

"Being a single parent, Mal, having to work *and* take care of a child all on your own… We were exhausted when there were two of us."

Meeting his gaze, she took him on.

"I grew up with a single mom who not only worked and tended to me but regularly opened our home to other children, as well. Troubled children."

He knew her history, starting with the high-end prostitute mother who'd tried to keep her but who'd eventually realized what her life was going to do to her daughter and had given her up. Mallory had been almost three then. She didn't remember the woman who'd later died of AIDS, contracted after Mallory's birth. She remembered having to be tested, though, just to make certain she wasn't carrying the HIV virus.

By the time Mallory went in the system she'd been too old to be immediately grabbed up like a newborn. There'd been a couple who'd wanted her, though. And after almost a year in the courts while living in their home as their foster child, they'd gotten pregnant on their own and changed their mind about the adoption.

She remembered them.

And then Sally had come into her life. A social worker in another county, who had her own professional caseload of children, Sally was also a licensed foster parent in the county where Mallory had been living. She'd taken Mallory in and kept her until she'd gone off to college. There'd been children in and out of their home during the entire time she'd been growing up, but she'd been the only permanent foster Sally had had. The other kids had been like a shared project between them, with the two of them doing what they could to love the foster children during the time they were in their home.

Mallory had always loved caring for kids. Nurturing came naturally to her. She was meant to be a mother.

"Have you talked to Sally about this?" Braden asked. He'd met the woman a couple of times, but she'd retired, moved to Florida, met a man and married— her first marriage, late in life. He had a big family that she'd taken on as readily as she'd taken in all those children over the years.

"Not yet," she said. "But I'll let her know at some point. You know she's going to tell me to adopt, rather than birth, and while you'd think, in my position, having grown up as I did, that I'd be looking in that direction, I just want a biological family of my own."

"So find a man to share it with you."

Her heart lurched. And quieted. She shook her head.

"You've hardly dated, Mal. I'd hoped that guy at Thanksgiving—that dad—was someone you were getting interested in."

"I have dated," she told him. And she listed four men in three years. He nodded as each name rolled off her tongue. She'd told him about every one of them. "There's been no spark." She could have left it there, but for some reason, didn't.

"You know as well as I do, Bray. The magic is so great in the beginning, but there's no guarantee it will last. Look at us. Tragedy happened. You changed, I changed, or we found different parts of ourselves that hadn't had reason to present before." She shook her head. "I just don't trust the whole magic, in love thing. Besides, you said yourself many times that I changed even before tragedy hit. I loved motherhood more than I loved being a wife."

His words, not hers, but she wasn't sure they were wrong. She'd loved being his wife more than she could ever put into words. And yet, being a mother…it was like an empty cavern inside of her had suddenly been filled to the brim.

"The Bouncing Ball takes up twelve hours a day of your time."

She was proud of her daycare. It had a waiting list now, since she'd made the news the previous summer when a couple come to her for help in finding their kidnapped child. She was even, at Braden's suggestion, raising her rates for new clients. She'd put her foot down when it came to charging her current clients more.

"I spend my days taking care of children, Bray," she said now. "And I have a fully trained and certified staff who also specialize in child development."

Yes, she spent twelve hours a day at the center, doing what a mother does. Now, instead of just doing it for other people's children, she'd be doing it for her own, as well. And then getting to spend the remaining twelve hours a day doing the same.

"There'll be no more empty hours," she said aloud.

Braden seemed to be searching for words, and for the first time in a while she hated what they'd become. Hated the friendship that kept so much inside, erecting an invisible and completely safe barrier between them.

"Tell me what you're really thinking." She blurted the words.

And, of course, their waitress chose right then to deliver their dinner.

She could hardly eat. But because he was devouring his steak, she forced herself to go through the motions. Was she being way too insensitive here? Telling her ex-husband that she was having a baby when the loss of their own child was what had driven them apart?

Telling him she was having a baby when she knew he blamed himself for their loss?

"You wanted me to move on," she said, putting down her fork when she couldn't pretend to eat anymore. "More and more I can feel your tension, Bray. You need me to get a life."

"I never said that."

"You didn't have to."

He didn't deny her accusation.

"I'm right, aren't I? You feel responsible for my unhappiness, which means you can't move forward until I do."

Putting a forkful of meat in his mouth he chewed. His lack of response infuriated her. And yet, not as much as it might have done six months ago. Just because Braden didn't respond didn't mean he had no response.

"SIDS is not something you can predict," she said. "And if we'd been home, Tucker still would have died."

That's what the doctors told her. And the counselors. She still didn't totally believe it. If she'd been home, if Braden hadn't pressured her to leave their son with a nanny so that he could have some one-on-one time with her and spend most of the night making love with her, she might have heard a change in his breathing on the baby monitor. Might have been able to get to him in time.

To do what, she didn't know. At least she could have had a chance to breathe her own air into him.

To hold him.

Feeling herself sliding backward, she took a sip of wine. Four years of counseling, of recovery, and then she could so quickly be right back there.

"If you'd really believed we did nothing wrong by being gone that night," he said, "you'd have been able to have sex with me in the months that followed."

His softly spoken words hit her with a ferociousness she knew he hadn't intended. She sat back, hands shaking, trying to get control of emotions that just didn't die.

Her inability to want sex with him, even after the immediate blow of grief had worn off, had been a final nail in their marriage's coffin.

Their lovemaking the night Tucker died had been incredible. She'd even admitted, sometime during it all, that Braden had been right to insist that they have that time alone together. She'd missed him so much. Had half forgotten how incredible he made her feel, how right it was to be locked body to body with him, riding the crazy crest together.

And afterward…

"I felt so guilty for being so into you that I'd actually forgotten about him, on and off, for those hours when we were together. I was having the orgasm of my life while he was dying."

She could feel the tears pooling in her eyes and knew she'd gone too far.

She expected him to motion for the bill and almost reached for her purse.

"You aren't supposed to think about your children in the middle of sex, Mal. Or be turned on when you're thinking about them. It's a God thing, I'm sure. A shut-off valve that's embedded in us to keep the parent-child relationship sacred and on track."

She stared at him. Had he just said that? Were they really having this conversation?

Now? After all this time?

"My current concerns don't stem from anything to do with me," he told her then, getting them back on topic.

She sat back, the threat of tears gone. "I'd like to hear them," she told him honestly.

He cut a piece of steak, ate it. She broke off a piece of bread, played with it, making a pile of crumbs on her plate.

"I'm worried about you being alone and facing all of the things that could possibly go wrong."

"You don't think I'm strong enough to deal with life on my own?" That was a new one to her. She'd grown up in foster care, caring for foster children. She knew a hell of a lot about what could go wrong.

"I do. It's just that when it comes to mothering, Mal, you're so all in, and losing Tucker just about killed you. The idea of you having another baby… I figure it needs to happen for you, but are you sure you're ready? And doing it alone. What if—"

She shook her head. "No what-ifs, Braden. Not unless you want me stuck with no life forever. There are always what-ifs. I've chosen to tackle them one by one as they come, if they come. As a part of living."

He put down his fork, not quite through his steak. He'd barely touched the potato.

"You've really thought this through," he said, meeting her gaze head on.

"For months," she told him. "Remember last November I told you about Tamara referring that man to my daycare whose mother had died in prison giving birth, and he suddenly found himself with custody of a newborn without even knowing that his mother had been pregnant?" This was how she'd practiced telling him how she'd arrived at her decision.

This was what Braden would understand.

He nodded. "I kind of thought you and he would hook up."

"Tamara tried her best to get me to think that way, for a minute or two. I knew all along she had a thing for the guy."

Her friend had been unable to so much as hold a baby, however, which had definitely been a major roadblock for the couple. Still was, sometimes. But they were working on it. And there was no doubt in anyone's mind that Tamara loved that baby girl. Mallory could see it when Tamara came in to The Bouncing Ball, sometimes with Flint, sometimes not, to pick up little Diamond Rose after work.

"The thing is I've learned from seeing her courage, seeing how she forced herself to fight her way out of hell to give herself a chance to be happy, to make others happy. I have to do this, Braden. I can't let the past prevent my future."

Which was why she'd agreed to spend the previous Christmas on a yacht with some old friends from college instead of with Braden, as they'd done in the past. He'd gone home to North Carolina to be with his mom and sister, but up to the last minute had tried to get her to go with him. He'd been worried about her spending the holiday alone.

It hadn't been her best Christmas, but she'd done just fine.

"Okay." Hands on the table, he looked at her. Then loosened his tie and motioned for the check.

"Okay, what?"

"Okay, you're going to do this."

Her smile broke through with more of a rush than the tears. "And I have your support?"

"Of course. I told you the day we divorced that you'd always have that. It wasn't conditional, Mal."

Tears filled her eyes. "Thank you." She nodded and left him sitting there, credit card in hand.

Because she knew that was the way he'd want it.

Chapter Three

Holy hell, Mallory's going to have a baby.

Up at one in the morning, walking naked to the kitchen of the upscale high-rise condo he'd purchased on the beach not far from the harbor, Braden couldn't get the thought out of his brain.

He'd gone straight to his office after dinner to look over figures that had been coming in for a couple of days regarding his real estate interest north of L.A. He'd put out a contractor bid request and was going over every submission line by line. He'd put a call in to his architect, too, the same man who'd designed the complex where Braden Property Management had first begun and still resided. Some changes would be needed to suit the L.A. property, but the basic plan would be the same.

And it would bear the same name: Braden Property Management. Once upon a time he'd envisioned his second big venture to be titled a bit differently: Braden and Son Property Management. Once upon a time.

He hadn't told Mallory about his move. Hadn't even realized that he hadn't told her until after the check had been paid and he was heading out to the parking lot.

Holy hell. Mallory's going to have a baby. Alone.

He'd been prepared for her dating. Getting serious. Eventually marrying. All of which would have led to a very different future for her. Then he'd have prepared for her having another family. One that worked for her this time.

At thirty-three she was getting closer to her biological safety zone. She hadn't brought up that point at dinner but he was certain it had been on her mind. She was a child-development guru and firmly believed that her best chances for conceiving a healthy and robust child were before she turned thirty-five. Back in their other lives, she'd hoped to have at least two and maybe four by then.

Always in evenly numbered increments. She didn't want a family with an odd man out.

In his know-it-all, youthful arrogance, each time she'd mentioned her "clock goals" he'd pointed out that women were having babies successfully in their forties now. His way of deflecting the tension she'd begun to bring to their marriage after three years of still using birth control. They'd been establishing their businesses, and both had wanted to wait for children until they were secure.

It might have been more manly to deal with the tension. To acknowledge the validity of her feelings and sit with her as she felt them.

Sit with her. She wasn't the only one who'd had some counseling after Tucker's death. *Sit with her.* It had been what his counselor had told him he should have done when Mallory's grief had flooded their home to the point that he'd had to escape.

He hadn't been able to fix things. Hadn't known how to help. What to do.

What she'd apparently needed was for him to sit with her. Just be there while she grieved. *Be willing to be in her grief with her.* Whatever that meant. He got the words but he'd never completely figured out the concept.

Nor the next one. *Let her into your grief.*

The whole counseling thing hadn't lasted very long.

Wandering to his desk instead of heading back to bed, he sipped from his milk and stood in front of his computer—an identical setup to the one he had at his office and linked to it.

But work wasn't calling him.

Insemination was.

For a few minutes, earlier that night, he'd been with the old Mal. The one who didn't carry grief with her everywhere she went. From the way her eyes had lit up, even the way she'd held herself, it had seemed at first that he'd been sitting with the woman who'd blown his life away with her beauty, her contagious good feeling. He'd been in love all over again, there, for just a second.

For just a second he'd forgotten that he'd robbed her of the chance to kiss her baby good-night for the last time. To change him for the last time. Bathe him. Feed him. Hold him. Rock him to sleep. That had all been done by the nanny.

The next morning, the coroner had already been to the house by the time they'd arrived home. And Mallory's breasts had been leaking Tucker's food all over the place.

No matter how many times you relived it, the picture was always the same. He sipped his drink.

For just a second, earlier that night, Mal had seemed to be soaring again, instead of sagging.

He couldn't take that from her. No matter what misgivings he might have. No matter how valid they might be.

He was still staring at his computer, his milk almost gone.

If he was going to support Mallory in this venture, he needed to know everything there was to know.

Heading off for some boxers he came back and set to work.

An hour later, he had her on the phone.

"Braden? It's two in the morning! What's wrong?"

"You never said when you were going for your first procedure." *Or what kind it was going to be.* "For all I know, it's first thing in the morning. I wanted to chat a second before it happens."

"Tomorrow's Saturday," she reminded him. "My appointment's on Monday, after work, unless I don't ovulate as expected."

Not that far off, then.

"I called tonight's meeting. When were you planning to tell me about this?"

Whoa, buddy. You don't sound like a friendly and supportive ex-husband.

"Before tonight…or last night, now," she said. "But when you called Wednesday, asking to meet, I figured Friday night was fine."

He moved on, letting himself slide on the over zealousness of his questioning due to the lateness of the hour and shock of her news.

"I assume, given the circumstances, your ability to

conceive, your age and your excellent health that you're considering either ICI or IUI," he said, looking at the screen of statistics in front of him. Intracervical insemination. Intrauterine insemination. And there was intravaginal, too.

"Really, Braden? At two in the morning?"

"IVI is cheaper, by far, less invasive and less painful, but chances of conceiving the first time are considerably lower. ICI is still cheaper and less uncomfortable. But IUI has a slightly higher success rate. I think you should go with that. The less raised hopes and disappointment here the better."

"I'm fully prepared for this to take several months."

She yawned. And sounded slightly amused, too.

It *was* two in the morning.

His nearly naked body yearned during the second it took him to remind himself that it was Mallory he was talking to. The woman who had no interest in being a wife once motherhood was in the picture.

Mallory, who'd been unable to feel any desire for him at all since their son died.

Because she felt guilty for how great it had been for her that night.

That was new knowledge that he'd process at some point.

That night had been the best sex of his life, too. He didn't feel bad about that.

"How about a meet-up sometime this weekend?" he asked.

"Fine." Another yawn.

"I'm taking the boat out on Sunday," he told her. "You want to go fishing?"

"I'd rather lie on the deck and soak up some spring sunshine."

Right. He knew that. She'd gone out with him plenty of times. She'd never caught a fish and had only tried once or twice after he'd bugged her to the point where she'd given in.

If she had a boy, who was going to teach the kid to fish?

Knowing Mallory, she had some kid's fishing development group already lined up.

"Seven too early for you?" They'd have plenty of time on the boat for talking.

"Nope."

He could tell her about his L.A. plans, too. "Meet me at the dock?"

"Yep."

"Okay. We can—"

"I'm going back to sleep now, Braden. Good night."

He caught her chuckle just before the call went dead.

In leggings, a short-sleeved, oversize black shirt and tennis shoes, her dark hair tied back in a ribbon, Mallory boarded the fishing boat Braden had already owned when she'd met him eight years before. She carried a plastic bowl of cut fruit in her hands.

He was on board with a plate of doughnuts.

Looking at each other's goods, they laughed. "Some things don't change," she said, not as worried as she might have been about spending leisurely time with her ex-husband.

Surely, after three years of successful friendship, she and Braden could handle a few hours alone on the ocean. He probably wouldn't even leave the harbor.

He'd set a lounger for her on the deck, maybe the same lounger she'd used in the past.

She'd brought her own towel and dropped it on the lounger while he did what he did with his bait.

She opened the food, set it out on one of the benches with the little disposable plates, napkins and plastic forks she'd brought. He started the engine, fixed himself a plate and backed away from the dock. The boat had a little cabin and, noticing the travel mug he had next to him at the helm, she went below, found the coffee he'd made and poured herself an insulated cup full. With doughnuts and fruit on a plate, she pulled on the hoodie she'd brought aboard and settled in her lounger. When the sun was fully above them, she'd be hot, and she'd take off the hoodie and get some color on her skin.

And at some point, Braden was going to want to talk. Apparently to make certain that she knew she was doing the right thing and to tell her he was seeing someone again, she supposed.

Which was fine.

She'd listen, as she always did, and support him in his endeavors, as she always did.

Until then, she was going to relax into the bliss.

"Can you come up here?"

Drifting off to sleep, the rising sun's warmth cozy in the cool San Diego spring air, Mallory heard Braden. Not in the mood to hear about his new girlfriend, she took a second to decide whether or not to acknowledge that she'd heard.

The engine had stopped. She'd heard him moving around, getting his rod and casting his line. He'd be sitting up on the bow, watching the boats on the horizon as much as anything. She'd always said he did more relaxing than fishing when he went out, but hadn't seen that as a bad thing.

Thinking he had to carry the whole world on his shoulders as he did, Braden didn't relax enough.

And then she quit picturing it. Braden on the bow of the boat, wind in his air, was just…hot. A part of them that had to be dead to her now.

"Mal?"

"Yeah, I'm coming," she said, repositioning her sunglasses as she opened her eyes. They'd only been out half an hour. So much for her bliss.

But, hey, by the following night she might be pregnant. Braden could get remarried and it wouldn't be enough to snap her out of her good mood.

Joining him on the bow and sitting with her back propped on the small rail, she faced him, her feet in front of her with knees bent. His jeans and tennis shoes were new since they'd been divorced. The forest green T-shirt she'd washed before. A breeze blew his hair and he didn't seem to notice.

It made him look free. And just a touch wild.

The impressive breadth of his shoulders…that was the same as it had always been.

"You said you wanted my support in this venture of yours."

She wouldn't call having a baby a "venture" but understood that he would. And that what he called it didn't have to matter to her anymore. She nodded.

"Then I have some concerns I'd like to address."

He wasn't going to spoil her good mood. Not that he'd ever want to. Or intend to. He was trying to help. She got that.

"What are they?"

Throwing up one hand, he glanced at the line hanging placidly over the front of the boat.

"Most of them—" He stopped and shook his head.

"There's one major one, but I have a plan that can tend to it."

Did Braden just have a hitch in his voice? Heart beating faster, she studied her ex-husband. This mattered to him.

A lot.

Which warmed her. A lot.

"What's your plan?"

He frowned. "I'd like to present the concern before I move forward to the solution."

Had they been married, she'd have felt rebuked. She smiled, instead, finding his predictability, his need to keep things in order and under wraps, kind of endearing. "Of course."

"I'm concerned about the Y component," he told her, catching her completely off guard. She'd been expecting something more along the lines of her being a single parent. Taking on a two-person job all alone. Concerned that if she had a son, the boy would have no father figure.

Or anyone to take him fishing.

"You won't know family history," he continued, when she decided silence was the best answer until she could figure out where he was going with the conversation. "According to the National Human Genome Research Institute there are forty-eight known and listed genetic disorders that could be passed on to your child. That doesn't include the ones that occur when certain genes meet with inhospitable partner genes. If that were to happen, your likelihood of miscarriage would increase greatly, but I'm not even there yet."

It sounded like he was right there. Some more of her bliss faded. She wouldn't let go, though.

She was going to do this.

"Women have been having healthy donor babies for decades."

"And they've been having children with disabilities, too."

"So have married couples." So could they have had.

"But at least when you know the Y component, you have more of a chance to prevent something or to catch it in its earliest stages."

She didn't have an immediate answer to that. Except what she'd already said.

"You've been through so much, Mal. I applaud what you're doing here. I'm elated to see you taking up the reins of your life again. Moving on. Creating a future where you'll be happy."

Elated and *Braden* weren't words she'd put together. At least, not since Tucker died. Before that she'd seen some elation. More than he'd probably realized. But not as much as after she'd found out she was pregnant.

Was the pregnancy what had changed him? At least somewhat? Was there more to their divorce than just their dichotomous ways of dealing with life's tragedies, which ultimately blew their emotional trust in each other?

"I'm concerned, Mal," he said after a lengthy silence had fallen. "Really concerned. All weekend, the more I think about it, the more concerned I get. To the point that I'm not sure I can give you my support. Not with such a huge unknown."

So she'd do it alone. She'd already made that decision. And she'd known from the beginning that she might not win his buy-in.

Still, she could feel the weight of sadness come back, trickling into the outer recesses of her heart.

"I'm worried about what you'd do if you lost a second

child." The depth of compassion in his tone was something she hadn't heard in a long, long time.

"There are never guarantees, Braden. He or she could be hit by a car or a bolt of lightning. The point is, I'm not going to let the past rob me of my future."

Which was exactly what she'd told Tamara she shouldn't do.

Exactly when the words had become her mantra, she didn't know. She just knew that she felt the truth on a soul level.

"But why play with fate when you have a choice?"

Again, she had no ready answer so she thought about what he was saying, instead. She'd asked for his input. Having his support meant more than him just agreeing with everything she said and did.

She valued his opinion and she wanted him to care enough to speak up.

"You need a full family medical history," he said. "Or as complete of one as you can get. Way more than the general things the sperm bank provides. You need to know if his grandfather was prone to anxiety attacks or his entire family were unmotivated sloths."

"Right, so what do you suggest I do, Bray? Put an ad in the paper for sperm that comes with that kind of extensive history?"

"Of course not."

"Then what?"

It was only when she asked the question that she remembered he'd said he had a solution to her problem. A plan that would tend to his concern.

"You let me be your donor."

A wake from an incoming cruise ship in the distance hit the boat and she grabbed the rail, holding on so tight her knuckles turned white.

Chapter Four

She was staring at him, clutching the rail, mouth open, looking at him like he'd lost his mind.

He hadn't. Exactly the opposite, in fact.

He had to do this. He might not want to do it. Didn't like the messiness.

But he had to do it.

He owed it to Mallory.

"You're already going to be fighting the fear of another loss," he said, keeping things practical because he knew that was the only way to get through this. Through any tough situation. "You'll need all of the reassurances you can get. During your first pregnancy, you worried about the fact that you don't know your own family history. Knowing mine helped calm those fears."

She'd closed her mouth but was still staring.

"It's not conclusive that genetics have any link to SIDS, but we know that there is no evidence of it whatsoever in my family."

Shoulders drooping, she'd lost all appearance of happiness. Though that was not his goal, it was often the outcome whenever they had a real conversation. Still, he couldn't drop this.

"There are no guarantees, Mal, we both know that, but I'm as close to a guarantee as possible when it comes to healthy genes."

After Tucker's death, he'd had complete genetic testing done on himself, including familial screening, which he'd paid for. The results had shown that he and his family had absolutely no predispositions for any of the maladies such tests could indicate. He'd shared the news with Mallory.

And it had been the absolute wrong thing to do at the time. She'd taken his information to mean that she was to blame for their son's death.

"We also know that our reproductive environments are compatible." They'd conceived Tucker the first month they'd tried. "The sooner you conceive, once you start trying, the less stressful that portion of the process will be."

He saw her blink and took that to mean she was hearing him.

"Further down the road, if the child were to develop an illness or sustain a severe injury, something that needed a blood transfusion or donor of any kind, you'd have both parents to pull from."

She let go of the rail, wrapped her arms around her knees and looked out to sea. Was she going to turn him down?

"We can get everything drawn up legally," he continued, figuring that he'd covered all of the bases in his mind since Friday night, and if he just kept talking, he'd allay any concerns she might have. "You'd be the sole parent, just like you want. I'd have no say in anything, no legal rights, no more than any anonymous donor."

He drew from the thoughts that had consumed his weekend. "It would save you money, as well," he said. "You wouldn't have to pay for the sperm."

Her glance, when it swung back his way, had his heart palpitating for a second. He wasn't sure why.

"You're actually suggesting that we have sex?" The sentence ended almost on a squeak. He wasn't sure if she was offended or simply appalled and shocked.

At least she'd spoken.

"Of course not," he quickly reassured both of them. Yeah, he'd been cursed with an apparently lifetime attraction to his ex-wife, but she cringed at the idea of sex with him, and there that possibility ended. "I'd leave my specimen at the clinic, but I'd do so as a non-paid donation specifically for you."

She'd have to pay for the procedure, just not the sperm.

"If you go with IUI your chances of conceiving the first time would be better than with sex."

Mallory was shaking her head.

"What?"

"Do you realize the mess we'd be making if we did this?"

Sitting on the bow of his boat, her little feet in ridiculously small-looking tennis shoes, the woman made him nuts and peaceful at the same time. Helping Mallory was the right thing to do. Tucker would have expected it of him.

Hauling her downstairs to bed was not even in the realm of possibility.

Nor did he want it to be, anymore. Sex with Mallory came with a whole knotted ball of strings attached.

"That's the beauty of it, Mal," he said, glancing over as his fishing line grew taut. There'd be no fish there. He hadn't baited the damned thing.

He could just imagine being in the middle of presenting his case and having to stop to reel in a slippery, smelly, great-tasting piece of fish.

"We're in complete control here, Mal, and we've got the perfect vehicle. We've spent three years building a friendship that would allow the peace of mind you need for this venture. It couldn't be better if we'd planned it all along."

"We live on the surface," she said. "A baby won't stay there. Nor will all of the emotions attached to having one. I'm fully prepared for that. Are you?"

She wasn't getting it. "That's just it! I won't be emotionally involved. I'll be going on with my life, as planned, while providing you the means to go as safely as possible on with yours."

Frowning at him, her eyes only partially hidden by her sunglasses, she said, "You honestly think you can father a child without feeling anything?"

Sure, there'd be some feelings attached, at first probably, until he fully adjusted to the changes in their lives. "No more so than any other sperm donor."

"They don't ever know if their sperm is even used, let alone have a relationship with the recipient."

"Some do." He'd researched that one. "Men donate to gay women friends. Women are surrogates for gay men friends. I read about a man who donated to his best friend, who was celibate, so he and his wife could have a baby. And a mother who carried for her barren daughter and son-in-law—"

"We were married, Bray. We had a son together. Lost

a child together. And you think you can father my second child and just walk away?"

"I do." He really did. "When I'm ready to have a family of my own, I know full well I can do so. I'll meet a woman, the desire will be there and I'll have my family. I'm not there yet. But you're ready to have your family, and I can help ensure that you have the best chance at doing so happily." He didn't waver as he met her eye to eye. The plan made perfect sense.

"I need your support during the pregnancy more than I need the sperm," she said. "Sperm I can buy. But you're right, it's going to be hard. I've done all the reading, too, and giving birth after SIDS is hard. Your head plays with you, makes you afraid what happened before can happen again. I blame myself, like my body is broken somehow because it produced a child with a faulty breath regulator. What I was hoping to have from you was the common sense reminders that calm my fears."

"And you'll have them."

"It would be much easier for you to give them with more detachment," she said, the steady look in her eye and the calm tone of her voice making him listen to her. "Having no intimate involvement will better ensure you getting through this with the least amount of discomfort. You know, if the child isn't yours..."

"He won't be mine in an emotional or legal sense," he said immediately.

She was making a point. He got it. When the kid was born, wouldn't Braden need a second chance, too?

He shook his head, adjusted his baitless pole. "I'm giving away my sperm, Mal, not becoming a father." The designation was key. "It's all in how you process it."

But if she truly didn't want his biological component in her child...if, in spite of the testing he'd had done, she still thought his genes were partially to blame for what had happened, then he wouldn't force her. Couldn't force her. And he didn't even want to try. He just wanted this to work out for her. Most of the process was completely out of his control, except for this one small area where he could possibly positively affect her chances.

"Can I think about it?"

Her question came right when he was giving up.

"Of course."

"On the deck? In the sun?" She was already crawling her way off the bow, giving him too good a view of her ass as she did so.

Way too good.

Hard in the wrong place, he set about baiting his line. It was time to do some real fishing. And not for the things he couldn't have. Or things that no longer existed.

Weak in the knees, Mallory made it back to her lounger without incident. Sinking into the woven chair, she kept on her sunglasses just in case Braden was looking. And she refrained from wiping the tears from her cheeks for the same reason.

She'd just been given a second chance. From the minute she'd met her ex-husband she'd known that she'd wanted him to be the father of her biological family. To someone who'd grown up an orphaned foster kid, whose own mother hadn't even known who'd fathered her, biology was important.

So important.

As important as Braden Harris was to her.

She couldn't let him do this. Couldn't use him this way. It was his guilt playing with him. She knew that.

Just as she knew that keeping your baby in your room was a key SIDS preventative. She'd studied them all, from the Mayo Clinic to the American Academy of Pediatrics and every blog or message board she could find in between:

Place baby on back, not side or stomach.

Remove all fluffy bedding.

Keep crib as bare as possible.

No prenatal smoking.

Good prenatal care.

Pacifier at night after four weeks of age.

Breastfeeding.

And baby in your own room for a minimum of six months, better if it was twelve.

Not in your bed but in your room. It had to do with waking more easily, among other things. Logic then followed that if she'd been home that night Tucker would have been in his smaller crib in their room, where he'd been every night since his birth. She'd have been there, too. Which could have prevented SIDS.

Braden had done his own reading. He had to know this, too. And he was offering to give her what she wanted in order to appease his guilt.

Maybe it would be kindest to give him a way to atone and move on.

How could she put him through fathering a child he didn't want? How could she ask him to experience the pregnancy with her, knowing what it would probably cost him? How could she hurt him any more than he'd already been hurt, loving him like she did?

Unless…if atoning set him free…

She tried to doze, to let the sun take her to the peaceful place outside of pain, and ended up thinking about Tucker instead. The sound of him laughing. The first time he'd laughed Braden had been at work. She'd been alone with the baby, coming at him again and again with funny noises, stopping just short of reaching him to pull back and start again, reveling in the way his eyes had followed her every movement.

Braden had missed the whole thing. Tucker had been asleep when he'd arrived home that evening and though Braden had gone to wake him, she'd told him not to. It would have been too hard to get the baby back down. Feeling as sleep deprived as she had been, the admonition hadn't been completely without warrant, but what would it have hurt in the long run? Yeah, she'd been exhausted, but it wasn't like she'd had to get up to go to work. She'd still had another month of leave ahead of her. Even if the baby hadn't laughed again that night, Braden would have racked up more minutes of memories to feed him in the years that followed.

Someone like Braden probably wouldn't access those memories like she did. And when they came to him, calling up a wealth of emotion, they might be more a hindrance than anything else.

So maybe someone like Braden, someone who was happier shutting out emotion than letting it in, would be the perfect sperm donor—if he really didn't want another child of his own.

But what if he only thought he didn't? What if, once they got into it, once she heard a heartbeat and then started to show, once the baby started to kick, he found out he really wanted it all again, too?

She tried to find the idea abhorrent but couldn't.

Because if Braden could be the man she'd thought he was, there'd be no more perfect scenario than having his baby.

Which was the true problem, she acknowledged, lying there with her eyes closed, the sun beating down on her, the gentle sway of the boat rocking her.

The real problem was her. What if she got pregnant, heard the heartbeat, started to show, felt the baby kicking her…and wanted Braden to get excited about all of those things because it was his baby, too? What if she fell in love with him all over again?

What if she started to fall back into who she'd been? A woman who'd been ashamed to cry because her husband didn't like emotional outbursts. One who'd curtailed her most exciting moments when he was around for the same reason.

One who'd grown to relish her time alone with her baby so she could gush and be all intensely moved by the miracle of him and just feel complete.

No, she couldn't do it. Couldn't have Braden's baby.

That settled, she concentrated on the slow rhythm of the boat's movement and tried to drift off with it.

But she lay there, wide awake as a thought struck her.

She had to put the baby first.

Always.

In the end, she didn't matter at all. What mattered was her baby's health. His or her best chance at a long and happy life. Braden was right. With a sperm donor there were many unknowns.

She herself was an unknown, too. Yes, she'd had her own genetic testing and didn't carry any alarming signs, but her family might. She had no way of knowing if there was a history of cancer. Or liver or kidney disease. Or slowly developing areas of the brain that regulated breathing.

Not only could her baby develop something, but she could, too. What if kidney failure ran in her family? Or car accidents?

Sitting up, Mallory opened her eyes, taking a minute

to bring herself back mentally to where she was. The ocean. The boat. Fresh sea air and sunshine.

Car accidents weren't genetic.

But they did take people unexpectedly, leaving loved ones behind to fend for themselves.

In her case, it would leave her little one with no known family at all. He or she would be just like Mallory, a foster.

Rising, she made her way back to the front of the boat. Braden was sitting with his forearms resting on raised knees, looking in her direction. His line lay limp before him. There wasn't a single fish in the basket close by.

With a raised brow, he seemed to ask if she'd reached her decision.

"I have a question."

"Okay. If I don't have the answer, I'll see what I can do about finding it."

The reply was so Braden she almost teared up again. And smiled, too. He tried. He really, really tried hard.

"If something were to happen to me, would you be willing to take the child, to raise him or her?"

"Of course."

It wasn't so much his answer—which she'd have expected if she'd given herself enough time to think about it—as it was his lack of hesitation that set her suddenly frightened heart at ease.

"Then I accept your offer."

"Good."

He was looking at her. She looked back at him.

They'd just agreed she was going to have his baby.

And it felt as though they'd never been further apart.

Chapter Five

Feeling not the least bit relaxed, Braden gave up any pretense of enjoying a Sunday morning fishing jaunt. Mallory seemed to share his eagerness to get off the boat, based on how quickly she'd agreed with his suggestion that they head back to shore.

It was as though once they'd made their decision to give her another child, they couldn't stand to be around each other.

The idea was ludicrous, and yet, it held a strong ring of truth, as well. Strong enough that he couldn't just let things go as they were. If he and Mallory couldn't be friends, if he didn't have the access to help her out when she needed him, the entire point of his involvement was moot.

Luckily he knew exactly how to fix that problem.

"I never did tell you why I called Friday night's meeting," he said, planning to finally tell her of his pending move. He'd lowered the throttle and headed a little more slowly toward the private marina where his dock was located. In the seat next to him, she'd been silently watching their progress.

Now she glanced at him, waiting for him to continue. He wanted to know what she was thinking—a husband's desire, not a divorced friend's one. Cutting the throttle completely, he let them bob on the water.

"What's her name?" she asked. And then, before he could answer, she added, "And are you sure she'll be okay with this? Because if you need to reconsider, I fully understand."

Staring at her, he wasn't sure whether to grin or be pissed. About to embark on a huge and potentially frightening life change, considering the demons that would be on the trip with her, Mallory was sitting there thinking about him. Letting him off the hook.

Just as she'd always done.

Why the thought pissed him off, he wasn't sure.

Or maybe it wasn't her at all.

"There is no 'her,'" he said. But he didn't like how available that made him sound, so he added, "At least not at the moment. And when there is, in order to qualify, she'll need to be okay with the fact that my ex-wife has a child that is biologically mine and that I am her friend."

Yes. That was it in a nutshell. All clean, wrapped up and completely doable.

"She'll have to be one special woman." Her grin made him think of how special she was.

Right.

And, of course, any future relationship he might have would be with someone else who was special to him. That was the nature of hooking up. It would be that way whether he donated sperm or not.

"I can put off my appointment," she said, making him aware that he hadn't responded to her earlier comment.

The ocean's vastness called to him. And yet, there he sat in the harbor. The story of his life. At sea, but missing out on a world of possibility.

No. What was that nonsense? His life was a damned good story. He got up every morning, eager to get going. His work didn't just earn him loads of money; it energized him.

"I think you need time to seriously reconsider," Mallory said, turning that warm, concerned gaze on him. How well he recalled that look. He'd almost been jealous of his own son once, when he'd been trying to talk to Mallory about a particularly testy client and a lucrative deal that had almost gone sour, and instead of hearing him, she'd heard Tucker sneeze and had immediately turned that same look on the baby.

Hard to believe he even remembered that.

"It will just be too messy."

Whoa. She wasn't changing her mind, was she?

"Only if we make it so," he said, jumping in before the deal went south on him. "It will be what we make it," he continued, looking her straight in the eye. "We're friends. Your child will be your child, just as though you had an anonymous donor. I will be there for both of you, as a friend of the family, in the same way as I would be if you purchased the sperm." He'd spent much of the previous day getting straight with it all. "The only difference will be the biology—a scientific component that no one will ever need to know about—that will make you and the child safer than if you did it anonymously."

She still looked as though she needed reassurance.

"It's not like we just divorced," he said, putting every

ounce of confidence he had into his words. "We're three years in, Mal. We've got this down."

She nodded.

"If anyone can do it, we can."

She watched him, saying nothing.

"It's perfect for us, really," he said, continuing to fill the silence. "You said multiple times that I'm detached. So here's where my detachment works for us."

He hadn't been detached when they'd been married. But he was now. Somehow he'd become what she'd thought she'd seen.

"I still think I should cancel my appointment to give you more time."

"I don't need any more time. If you do, if you want to think about this some more, then by all means, post-pone things. But you don't need to do it on my account."

Her response was quick. "I'm not worried about me. My mind is fully made up."

"I meant about using me as a donor. If that's going to be a problem for you."

"I think it's fraught with potentially difficult situa-tions, most I fear that we can't even see right now, but, honestly, I'd take on any of them to have the peace of mind of knowing that if something happened to me, my child would have biological family willing to wel-come him."

"But he would only know about that biology if such an occasion arose." They needed that clear. They were proceeding as if this was an anonymous sperm donor. For her sake, more than anything. It was what she needed.

"Correct." She nodded but then glanced out to sea.

"Maybe you do need to take a little time," he told her, not wanting to rush her. Mallory had never been one to jump into anything. Because she gave her all when she got there.

She looked at him. "I told you, my mind is firmly made up."

He nodded, believing her.

"So, do you need me tomorrow, then?" He'd never been to a fertility clinic, but he'd heard his share of do-it-in-the-cup jokes. Seen sitcom episodes on TV. It wasn't his style, but what the hell.

"I thought I'd call in the morning and see what they suggest. With the change of plan, they might want to reschedule."

He met her gaze and held it. "So, I'm good. Are you?"

Her smile rocked him more than the incoming wake. "I'm good."

He wanted to believe both of them.

Mallory didn't contact Braden again until after she'd spoken with the clinic Monday morning. Because of the different procedure, they would need to reschedule if she took Braden up on his offer. Though they almost never sought each other during the business day, she took a quick break from The Bouncing Ball to ride the elevator up to the top floor. William, the receptionist who kept Braden Property Management running smoothly, looked surprised but not unhappy to see her.

"Mrs. Harris!" He stood, coming around the built-in counter to take her hand. She'd kept Braden's name. Her business had been established in that name. The hassle to change everything hadn't seemed worth it. Particularly since she had no ties, emotional or otherwise, to her maiden name. But the Mrs... Most people just called her Mallory. Or Ms.

"It's so good to see you," William's smile was genuine and his pleasure at her sudden presence gave her pause.

She shouldn't have broken her and Braden's unspoken protocol by showing up at his office suite. But the clinic only had a couple of openings. She had to call them back to let them know if she'd be keeping her afternoon appointment.

And she'd needed to see Braden one more time, to make certain that he knew what he was getting into before they did something irrevocable.

"Good to see you, too, William." She smiled back at the man who'd been with Braden since college and was more of an office manager than a receptionist. William just liked to be out front, keeping an eye on everything that went on. From out here he knew which agents were present, which mortgage brokers were on time and which clients appeared nervous when they arrived.

But he couldn't know why Mallory was suddenly visiting her ex-husband.

"Is he in?" she asked, nodding toward the hall that led to Braden's huge, luxurious office suite.

"An hour ago," William confirmed.

He didn't ask her to wait while he let Braden know she was there, but she knew he'd call to inform him she was on her way back.

"I'm sorry," she blurted as he opened his door just as she was approaching. "I shouldn't be up here, but—"

"Of course you should be up here," he said, closing his door behind her as she entered the rooms she'd helped him decorate.

They'd christened each one with lovemaking a long time before. An inappropriate memory to be having in that moment.

He motioned toward the couch in the main room—which also housed a massive teak desk, an entertainment center with a large-screen TV and a wet bar.

"I only need a second," she said, shaking her head at his offer to sit. "I have to get back."

He slid his hands in his pockets, drawing her attention down there. To the part of him that he'd be using on her behalf if they did this.

Oh, God.

Could they really be considering such an asinine choice?

Glancing up, she felt the heat rise up her neck to her face. He'd caught her looking.

Of course he would. Braden missed very little.

Unless it came to emotions. Then he managed to bypass pretty much everything.

Or at least he seemed to.

The man she'd married, the one with whom she'd shared the best years of her life, had shown her a different side. He'd been verbally reticent, not one to express emotion in words, but he'd definitely known them. And shown them. He'd also been able to sense even the slightest change in her, it had seemed.

At least that was the way she remembered it, looking back. Who knew how it had really been?

"I called the clinic," she said, hoping she sounded as confident as she wanted him to think she was. About the procedure, there was no doubt.

About using him, there was tons of it.

But knowing her baby would have family if something happened to her simply meant too much to her to decline his offer.

"And?" he prompted her.

"If we… If I… I'd have to reschedule," she found her

point eventually. "The procedure is slightly different. They have one opening on Wednesday morning and one Thursday, late afternoon. They need an immediate call back if I'm going to cancel this afternoon's appointment."

"'If?' Are you reconsidering again? I thought we'd been through all of that."

So much for her giving him time to change his mind. He wasn't being open-minded enough to do so.

"We have been. But I just don't think you realize what you're putting yourself in for. The possible ramifications. You'd have a child you could never acknowledge, Bray. Think about that. I mean, if we lived on opposite sides of the country, maybe that wouldn't be such a critical consideration, but I'm right downstairs. My baby will be right downstairs. Every single day."

Right now they didn't see each other on a daily basis. But knowing that he had a child so close and that he couldn't be a part of its life might drive him over the edge.

"Which brings me to the reason I called Friday's meeting," he said.

For a second there she thought he was losing it. He hadn't known her plans, nor made his offer when he'd called the meeting. What could one possibly have to do with the other?

"I'm confused."

"I'm moving, Mallory. So, you see, I won't be upstairs from the baby every day."

She went cold. From head to toe, everything about her was cold. She stared at him, trying to assimilate what he'd said.

She headed for his couch and sat.

"You're moving." It wasn't a question, and yet...he was moving?

When Braden sat next to her, closer than he'd ever been when alone with her since their divorce, she knew that his news was big.

Serious.

And it was coming at her whether she wanted it or not.

Just as she knew that she did not, in any way, want him to leave.

That one was as unequivocal as their divorce.

Chapter Six

"You own properties in several different cities now. Why would you have to move to purchase another?" she asked when he told her about buying the L.A. property.

She'd gone white. Braden hadn't expected that.

He'd figured she'd be upset at first. Mallory wasn't a huge fan of change. But she always saw reason. Always supported his choices. Encouraged them, even.

Perhaps he should have been a bit more conscientious in telling her his big news.

"I don't have to move to buy the L.A. property," he told her. "I want to move." Maybe that was it. He'd misrepresented the plan. He'd come at it from the business end of things. "The other properties all were purchases of existing buildings, with tenants," he explained. "The L.A. one is going to be like this one here, Mal. I'm going to make a second Braden Property Management building, starting from scratch. I'll be using renditions of the same plans. To anyone just driving by, the properties will look pretty much identical. I'll need to be on hand, much like I was here, during the entire process." He heard himself and corrected, "I want to be there."

"This building is your baby." She'd spoken softly, looking at him with that tender gaze that seemed to see more than was there. "And as such, you have my full support."

"I wouldn't put it that way."

"I mean…the new project is you building your own life separate and apart from me. Braden Property Management in San Diego, with The Bouncing Ball on the ground floor, is us, Bray. You love this place, but you need to make a life of your own. That's as it should be."

He shook his head. She was making way more of this move than was there. Except for one key point.

"I'm a developer," he said. "The project will be a challenge and I look forward to that," he agreed. "I also think maybe it's time for us to live far enough apart that we aren't in each other's spheres all day every day."

Her lips pursed, she nodded, then stood.

"That's it? You're just going to go?" he asked her.

"I have to get back downstairs," she reminded him. "I don't like to be gone long, you know that. And I have to call the clinic." She was walking toward the door. All he could see was her back.

He had to let her go. This was their life.

"Thursday afternoon would work better for me," he shot out at her.

She stopped, nodded, then reached for the door handle and was gone.

Leaving him, once again, feeling like a jerk.

* * *

Mallory was more excited than nervous—and eerily calm, too—for most of that week. Her plans were solid. Right. She had no doubt about that.

Just as Bray's new plans were right for him.

She didn't doubt that, either.

Hence the calm. Three years ago they'd chosen to live life on individual paths, rather than one path together. It had been the right choice for both of them.

No doubt on that score.

So why was she so incredibly sad all of a sudden? Not overall. Not all day. Or every minute. But in bouts. Unexpectedly throughout the day, for a minute or two.

L.A. was only two and a half hours away. Knowing Braden, he'd still be in San Diego at least once or twice a week. He wasn't going to leave the San Diego headquarters hanging.

Unless...

Was he planning to sell the complex? Would the new owner raise her rates to something she couldn't afford without passing on higher fees to her clients? Many of her clients worked in the building and couldn't afford any higher fees. Would some of the smaller businesses be forced to move? Would she?

She couldn't believe he'd do such a thing.

And yet, things were changing so drastically. She was taking very real steps to have a family again. To be a mother.

Braden was not only supporting her, but doing everything he could to make the way easier for her.

She had no business putting any kind of a guilt trip on him about his plans.

But maybe she was a little more on edge than she might have been when they met in the parking lot of

Braden Property Management Thursday after lunch. He'd suggested they drive to the clinic together. Considering the distance, she couldn't come up with a reason why they shouldn't. It made absolutely no sense to take two cars from San Diego all the way to Marie Cove.

Coming from work, he was still in his suit, looking confident—and too sexy for her immediate peace of mind. She'd changed from jeans and a Bouncing Ball polo shirt to a calf-length, colorful, flowing skirt and a short-sleeved, figure-hugging purple shirt with sandals.

The ladies who worked for her knew she had a doctor's appointment. They didn't know why. No one did. Not even Tamara.

When she was pregnant, she'd share her news. Until then, she needed to keep things low key.

They got in Braden's dark blue luxury SUV without discussing whose car they'd take. The vehicle was new since their divorce. She'd ridden in it a handful of times. The tissue holder attached to the passenger-side sun visor was one she'd purchased for him years before.

Kind of ironic, considering that her crying—and thus needing tissues—had contributed to the reasons for their divorce.

"Thank you for doing this," she said as he maneuvered through traffic and pulled onto the highway heading north.

The appointment ahead was bound to be awkward for him, going into a room with the express purpose of…

Yes, well, she wouldn't be there and needed to steer her mind away from that thought. He'd be having a somewhat personal medical procedure. Administered by himself.

Details not her concern. But she couldn't help thinking about that particular part of his anatomy. She knew it well. Had loved it well.

Again, not her business.

Her business came immediately after his. A short procedure. And then, by the time she was on the opposite side of that very highway later that afternoon, she could be pregnant!

She wouldn't know, of course. It would take a couple of weeks before she could hope for accurate results from a home pregnancy test.

"You nervous?" Braden asked as he set the cruise control and settled back.

"A little." Not as much as she'd have thought. She was creating her future, one step at a time. Just one step. That's all she was facing that day. That's all she'd ever have to face. One step. Before she'd have to deal with the next.

Or get to celebrate the next.

One thing she'd learned from losing Tucker, from the grief counseling, was to live in the moment. To enjoy every single moment as best she could. The moment was all anyone ever had at any given time. And then, God willing, they'd have another one moment.

They'd been on the road half an hour and said two words a piece.

"This isn't a bad drive," she offered. She'd made it a few times in recent months.

"No, it's not."

He'd obviously been making the trip, too, adding on the extra forty-five minutes further north to L.A. At least, enough to pick the property he was considering for his new venture.

Odd how their attempts to get on with their lives apart from each other had led them both to the L.A. area.

Difference being, of course, that she only visited. He was moving.

"Maybe we could drive by your new property," she offered, hoping he never knew how difficult it was for her to support him. She was being selfish and wasn't proud of that. "You know, when we're finished at the clinic. We'd be almost there and I'd like to see it."

More like she needed to know where he was going to be. Just so she could relax and let go.

He glanced at her. She could tell but didn't look over at him.

"I'd like that, actually, if you're up for it," he told her. "I'd like your input."

Warmth flooded her.

All of these changes were a good thing.

Maybe everything really would be okay.

Braden didn't need the magazine. He'd been apprised of its availability. Knew exactly where and how to access it, but didn't. All he had to do was picture Mallory their last night together, naked and wild in that hotel room, as hot for him as he had been for her.

The whole thing was over in less than a minute.

Which was a good thing, considering the night that did it for him was also the night their son had died.

She couldn't have sex again after that.

The memory of their time together that night turned him on. If that made him a sick bastard, then, he supposed it did.

For Mallory, the two were indelibly tied into one.

For him, they were two completely different things. For her, losing one meant losing both. In his mind, their togetherness as a couple could have been something that saw them through the loss.

But then, his tendency to live in his mind had been a big part of their problem.

He made business calls and answered email from his phone while he waited out in his vehicle for Mallory. He'd been told it could take six or more tries for her procedure to take. This was the only time he'd need to be present. He hoped it worked out for her quickly.

If this was what she really wanted.

Maybe after trying, she'd have second thoughts. This attempt wouldn't take, and she'd forgo another.

Maybe.

Staring at email he wasn't comprehending, Braden had to stop himself a second. Was he hoping Mallory didn't get pregnant?

Did he want this venture to fail?

He wanted her happy. That answer came to him quite succinctly and he recognized the absolute truth of it.

And if it took a baby to make her so?

He wished it didn't.

But if it did?

He wanted her happy.

Satisfied with where his internal dialogue ended, he answered three emails in as many minutes. One from an investor. Two from contractors regarding the L.A. property.

Mallory was making her new life.

He was making his.

She didn't look any different. Logically he'd known she wouldn't and yet, as Mallory climbed back into the passenger seat next to him just as the sun was starting to set, he was struck by how normal she looked.

As though he'd expected her to sprout horns or a baby rattle or something.

She strapped herself in and as the seat belt crossed over the front of her body, he remembered another time, another doctor's office parking lot. They'd just come from her thirty-nine-week checkup. She'd begun to dilate. They'd had an ultrasound and Tucker had been head down and in position. Mallory had been talking nonstop as she'd guided the seat belt beneath her belly bulge and clicked it closed.

He'd looked at the huge belly sticking out there and for the first time had had a sense that there was going to be another human being in his family. That stomach wasn't just Mallory's thing. Just something she wanted and would be great at. It was a human being, ready to join them.

Them, not her.

He'd been scared to death. Afraid of what the change would do to the "them" that worked so perfectly, in his opinion.

And afraid that he wouldn't be as great a dad as she'd be a mom. Afraid that he'd disappoint her.

He'd also been strangely elated. And uncomfortably moved. That bulge was about to become his son. Having never had a dad or a brother, that new male advent into his family had suddenly been huge. Visions of fishing and sports and doing business together had started to pop up at the most unexpected times.

They'd always made him grin inside. Lifted the weight of the loads he carried. He'd never had another man to step in and be the man of the house if the need ever temporarily arose.

"What?" Mallory's voice broke into his thoughts, bringing him back to the moment. She was looking at him, concern on her brow.

"What, 'what?'"

"You're staring at me. And you had a funny look on your face."

He could tell her the truth. But then things could get messy.

"I'm just wondering how it went," he improvised. It was the truth. He had been wondering about that, in the midst of the rest of it.

"Good," was all she said.

He wanted more.

But didn't ask.

Braden didn't say a whole lot as he pulled onto the vacant property he hoped would be the newest Braden Property Management acquisition, and put his SUV in Park. Motor still running, he kept the headlights on, shining toward the center of the property. It wasn't quite dark, but almost.

Mallory looked around, noticing the lake across the street. They'd just passed a gated community, and across the other way was a fine dining restaurant with green grass and landscaping that could have been on the cover of *Better Homes and Gardens*.

Just outside of L.A., it was the most spacious area she'd ever seen so directly attached to the crazily busy metropolis.

"It's perfect, Braden" The words didn't quite catch in her throat. Only because she got them out before the deluge of emotion hit.

His new place would be better even than the San Diego version. Of course. Braden was a lot wealthier now than he'd been then. The first building had gone up with loans, not investors.

"You really think so?" He was watching her and she looked back at him.

"I do."

Her eyes glistened, but she smiled.

Looking satisfied, he nodded. "I was thinking the front of the building would face south," he said, going on to describe his vision for the complex.

She added a few suggestions, which drew other ideas from him. All in all, they sat there for almost half an hour.

Mallory was proud of how well she managed.

His new life was going to be great.

And she resented the hell out of it for taking him away.

Because somehow over the past three years she'd become completely selfish where Braden was concerned. Counseling, both grief and marriage, had taught her to focus on herself—the only thing she could control or fix. Maybe she'd gone a bit too far with that.

"Do you think it's wrong, me having a child?" If they'd been sitting in a restaurant with people buzzing around them, or in the broad light of day, she might not have asked.

In the dark in the enclosed and private comfort of his vehicle, with jazz music playing softly in the background, the question slipped past the barriers that guarded their friendship.

"I wouldn't have participated if I did."

She'd probably known that. And wished she'd asked a different question. Maybe more to the point would have been, *Do you like the idea of me having a child?* Or, *Do you want me to have a child?*

No. Neither one of those worked.

Do you feel good about me having a child?

Maybe that one was more what she wanted to know.

Was he hoping, secretly maybe, that she wouldn't conceive?

Now she was treading on minefield territory.

"Are you planning to sell the complex in San Diego?" Sitting back, she stared at other headlights on the road in the distance and watched the rhythm of their passing, one after another.

"Of course not. Why would I do that?"

She shrugged. Trying to keep her tone even, noncommittal, she said, "You don't need two headquarters."

"Braden Property Management can have more than one office. It needs more than one, actually."

Thinking about what he did, all of the people who worked for him, she could see that.

"Is William going with you to L.A.?"

"No. I need him right where he is, doing what he does."

She could see that, too.

"Don't worry, Mal. Everything is going to remain exactly the same as far as The Bouncing Ball, and the entire complex for that matter, is concerned."

It wouldn't be the same without him there.

"I'll still be around, at least once a week, if not more," he continued.

So what, he was reading her mind now, like he used to do when they were one? Two parts of a same whole so closely entwined that they knew what the other was thinking.

When had that stopped? Traveling back in her mind, she tried to pinpoint exactly when she'd stopped knowing what Bray was thinking. Or when she'd felt as though he didn't get her anymore.

She landed…nowhere.

She was probably just too tired.

The day had taken more out of her than she'd thought. Not physically. The procedure had been mildly uncomfortable and over more quickly than she'd expected.

But emotionally.

If all went as expected, she was going to be a mother again. Maybe not this time. Or next. But soon.

And Bray...he was going to be a business owner again. Same plans, same look, same top floor. If not on the current property he was considering, then on one like it.

It was kind of ironic. It seemed like in moving on, neither one of them was actually doing that. They were doing just as they'd done in the past—only this time they were doing it separately.

Mallory had no idea what to make of that.

Chapter Seven

One step, one minute at a time. Mallory spent the next two weeks living her life only in the moment. She might be pregnant; she might not. Didn't do any good to dwell on it, either way. If she was, great.

And if she wasn't, she'd try again.

Braden might be leaving soon; he might not—depending on how quickly things came together for him. He was going. She just didn't know when. Watching for his parking spot to be empty didn't serve any purpose, either. It would be at some point.

They met for lunch once. He told her that he'd made an offer for the property he'd shown her. He still hadn't chosen a contractor, but he'd narrowed it down to two.

And he wasn't buying a place to live right away. He'd be renting a suite at the hotel half a block away at first, and then looking for something nearby to rent until he had the building up and running. He'd be keeping his condo in San Diego, regardless, and planned to be in town, at the Braden Property Management office, at least one day a week.

So, for all intents and purposes, not that much would change as far as the two of them were concerned. They rarely saw each other more than once a week anyway. And sometimes less than that.

Overall, she was doing just fine. If you didn't count those moments when she imagined the spare bedroom in her little house as a nursery or touched her stomach and thought about bonding with a new baby.

Oh, and the time she'd lain in the dark and thought about being uncomfortably huge with baby and not having Braden's back to prop up against. It had taken her half an hour to figure out that she'd use pillows instead. A body pillow. She'd picked one up the next day and she had started using it, too.

On the thirteenth day after her procedure she still didn't get her period. While that didn't mean she was pregnant, her nerves tingled with energy all day long and into the evening. So much so that when she was mixing a bowl of tuna salad for a late supper and a knock sounded on her front door, she jerked so hard tuna flew off her spoon onto the counter and wall.

She wasn't expecting anyone and didn't usually have people just stop by. In the jeans and purple Bouncing Ball polo shirt she'd worn to work that day, she left the mess and went to look out from the corner of the front window. Her house wasn't big, but it was in a nice, predominantly crime-free neighborhood. Still, she was a woman living alone.

And she might have a baby to protect.

The thought was right there.

She recognized the SUV immediately and pulled open the door.

"Bray? What's up?"

He'd been to her home. Had taken a look at it with her before she'd purchased it. But he didn't visit.

"I called first but you didn't pick up."

Her phone was still in her bag, where she'd dropped it before a late meeting with a prospective client couple expecting their first child. "It's still on silent," she said aloud, taking it out and holding the screen up for him. He didn't step in, just stood there in his suit and tie and held out a key.

"I'm heading to L.A. and just thought, with me moving down there, you should have a key to my condo. Just in case."

He was moving? At eight o'clock on a Wednesday night?

She reached for the key. "Your offer was accepted on the property?"

"Not yet, but I have every reason to expect it will be, I want my guys there Friday morning. We'll need to apply for permits and want to get that process going immediately."

Oh. The whole contractor thing, getting going on an actual formation of a building—making it real— had come fast.

He'd be out of town when she took the pregnancy test the next day. They hadn't talked about her plans, or his part in them, since the day they'd visited the clinic together, but he knew the process, the timing.

He knew that tomorrow was her big day.

And yet he chose that day to go to L.A. and buy his property. His statement couldn't be clearer: he was moving on.

Which was good, because so was she.

"When will you be back?"

"Friday night or Saturday."

Mallory blinked. "That's only two days."

Chin jutting, he nodded. The porch light was bright, putting his dark hair in a spotlight but leaving his face in shadow.

"So, you aren't moving yet."

His shrug was so…him. It left her needing more. "I'm not going to be moving much of my stuff, just some clothes and personal items, but since I'm keeping my place here, I figured I'd buy new there. When the time comes."

Made sense, she guessed, though she didn't think she'd like having two sets of belongings. She'd want the red sweater with the crop sleeves that didn't itch, and it would be in her other place. The truth settled on her, though. She was a homebody. Braden was not.

Maybe that had been part of their problem without either of them knowing it. Or acknowledging it if they had.

"Okay, well, I'm heading out," he said, leaning in to give her a kiss on the cheek. She almost turned her head and opened her mouth.

And she was shocked by the sudden instinct to do so.

Must be hormones.

If she was pregnant.

"Be safe," she said to his back.

"Always," he called with a raise of his hand and was gone.

Leaving her standing there holding his key, wishing she'd had that kiss.

He was going to be back Friday night or Saturday, but he'd brought her a key to his place. Presumably to be able to let someone in if he had a problem, needed service or something sprang a leak.

He hadn't said. She could only guess.

So, did that mean that he'd be back over the weekend but leaving again almost immediately?

She should have asked. The real Mallory would have asked. Friend-instead-of-lover Mallory couldn't.

Cleaning up tuna from the wall, she told herself that she didn't care where Braden lived as long as he was healthy and happy. Needing to keep herself that way, she ate. Then she worked on spring-into-summer decorations for the daycare reception. She liked to change them every month, to keep things feeling fresh and happy. Crafting of all sorts made her happy.

Twice she went in to the bathroom, thinking she might take the pregnancy test a day early. It wouldn't hurt anything. Worst case, she'd be out the money it would cost to buy more. Considering that she'd purchased a case of them off the internet because she could get them so much cheaper, she wasn't all that worried about buying more.

Twice she went back to the third-bedroom-turned-craft-room in her house without taking the test. Chances were it would come up negative, which would only upset her. Still, it could just mean that it was too early to take the test, not that she wasn't pregnant.

If it came up positive she'd get all excited and might then find out she wasn't pregnant because it had been too early to take the test.

Logic told her twelve hours shouldn't make that much difference.

Braden had left town without even wishing her luck for the outcome of a test he knew she'd be counting the hours to take.

That hurt.

There. She'd admitted it.

He didn't have to be personally invested or anything. He didn't need to care for himself whether or not the insemination of his sperm into her body had created a new life. But she'd hoped he'd care for her sake, no matter whose sperm she'd used.

He wouldn't be back until after she'd had a day to deal with the results. Either way, she was bound to be a bit emotional over them. Elation, disappointment... either reaction would most likely be intense at first.

And Braden had purposely taken himself away.

So typical. And why had she expected any different? Of course he'd be there in a heartbeat if she called. But his choice was to be absent.

Her intensity made him uncomfortable.

She cut and glued—burning herself on the glue gun—embellished, trimmed, embossed, traced, drew faces, even did a bit of calligraphy with big thick strokes. Pulling supplies from various white plastic drawers stacked all along one wall of the room, she had her eight-foot worktable filled with papers, cardboards and pencils in various colors, an electronic cutter, paints, hole punches in several shapes, plastic pieces for 3-D effects, and yet she still saw Braden everywhere she looked.

How could he be so present in her mind, even after three years of divorce?

It wasn't until she was lying awake in the middle of the night that it hit her. He'd left her his key. Something he'd never done before—and he'd certainly been out of town for longer than two days on numerous occasions.

He'd left her his key.

Giving her access to him when he couldn't be there.

It hit her like a warm breeze on a cool day.

He was staying connected to her in his own way. And that was good enough.

Or at least good enough for her to settle into sleep. If, deep down, she needed more, wanted more, she'd let that go.

It was a learning process.

One minute, one step, one day at a time.

Braden checked on his offer first thing Thursday morning. The owner had phoned in a positive response, but it wasn't yet officially accepted. He made arrangements with the hotel to secure a suite for a monthly rate, good for however long he needed it, and got himself settled in. It would be fine for now. He was going to be ungodly busy, not only with contractors and building details but with filling twelve floors' worth of office suites.

That's when it hit him that he should have a daycare on the first floor. Being able to offer on-site childcare at a reduced rate was a great selling point. One that Mallory had come to him with. He'd trusted her judgment and she'd been right.

So, morally, he owed her the opportunity to open a second business if she wanted it. Practically, he didn't see it. The Bouncing Ball in San Diego took up all of her time as it was. And with a new baby, she'd have even less time. He couldn't support her taking on any more. She'd be stretched too thin, get stressed and lose sleep and not be happy.

Mallory was Supermom. She'd only be happy if she had ample time to spend with her new baby.

If she got pregnant. When she got pregnant.

She could already be pregnant.

And if she was, she wouldn't be in any position to join him in opening a new business.

He knew how she was. He remembered the way she'd buzzed through every hour of every day spouting off crib prices, watching sales, conversing on anything baby. He knew more about differences in breast pumps than he'd ever need to know. He could do a pretty good commentary on the benefits of disposable diapers, the differences between brands, even the comparable pricing on them from local stores. He remembered the calm glow about her, the light in her eyes and the joy in her smile when she'd told him the first time around that they were going to have a baby.

He'd whooped right along with her, grabbing her up and swinging her around until they were both dizzy. He'd made sweet love to her, taking it easy, and yet finding no less fulfillment for having done so. She'd been so beautiful that night, more than she'd ever been. Being pregnant had completed her.

He'd been certain back then that having Tucker had completed them.

He'd been all caught up in her excitement. Letting himself get carried away with the emotion of it all. Had allowed himself to wallow in the emotional high.

But emotion was fickle. It misrepresented facts. Made things seem different than they really were.

A second daycare would provide more financial security for Mallory. She could hire someone to run it for her if she didn't want to split her time between L.A. and San Diego. She'd have him in L.A., able to pop downstairs and check on things for her.

He wasn't her husband anymore.

He had no right to make her decisions for her.

Which meant that he had to call her and make the

offer. If she asked for his opinion, as a friend, he'd talk over her choices with her.

Decision made, he watched the clock until the half hour she usually took her lunch break, then called her. He'd had her on speed dial since he'd got a smartphone. He'd seen no reason not to continue keeping her there when he switched to newer versions.

She didn't pick up. Not even when, fifteen minutes later, he tried a second time.

She'd have taken the test that morning. Not the previous evening. Not the next day. On this, Mallory would be following every dictate to the nth degree. She was determined and she'd do all she could to get her part exactly right.

She'd also be tending to the emotional struggles that having this baby would be sure to bring her. It wasn't going to be easy. Fighting off fears. But she'd do what it took to be happy. She was that strong.

Which was why he loved the heck out of her.

Since waking that morning he had, on and off in the back of his mind, wondered about the results. He knew she'd call when she was ready to share them with him.

She hadn't done that yet.

And she wasn't answering his call. Or calling him back.

His realtor did, though, with the news that his bid had been accepted.

Sliding his phone in his jacket pocket, Braden went out to start his new life.

Chapter Eight

Though it was a difficult choice, Mallory didn't take a pregnancy test Thursday morning. The morning was hard, and yet she'd been energized, filled with a renewed sense of purpose.

She'd been going at Mach speed so that she didn't have time to think about the fact that her ex-husband—one of her best friends—was making an offer that, if accepted, would take him away from her.

She didn't want to know if the test was negative. Not yet.

It wasn't critical, either way. They'd told her that, commonly, it took more than one try. She had enough money already put aside to pay for six attempts.

She just didn't want to be disappointed. Not on that particular day. Her mental and emotional health was something she managed carefully. It had been a tough battle for her—learning to be kind to herself. To expect enough of herself, but not too much. To accept that she didn't have super powers that made her more accountable than anyone else.

For moral support, she called Tamara, her other best friend, and asked for a lunch date.

They met at a diner on the harbor, Mallory in her jeans and polo shirt, Tamara in a slim skirt and fitted jacket that made her look more like a glamor model than an efficiency expert.

"So?" the auburn-haired beauty said, looking Mallory straight in the eye after their hug. "What's up?"

They hadn't even been seated yet.

"Bray's making an offer on a property in L.A.," she said. This was their way, their pact. Born from a desperation to own their own lives after grief. To have a full and happy life after the loss of a child. Or as much of one as was possible.

Having met in grief counseling, the two had been deeply drawn to each other—and away from the group. They were alike in so many ways—and different in a lot of ways, too. But their spirits…it was like they'd been sisters in another life.

Or, as Tamara had once claimed, their babies in heaven had become best friends and were angels tending to the mothers they'd left behind.

There was no subterfuge. And no holding back.

They were each other's nonmedicinal medication.

"He's moving," Mallory continued.

"He's moving? To L.A.?" Tamara's eyes were wide.

The hostess stepped up to seat them, so all Mallory got in was a nod, but she felt better already. Tamara would see through any self-lying she might be doing. By asking the right questions, she'd lead Mallory to the truth.

Just as Mallory had done for Tamara last fall when she'd held a stranger's baby and fallen apart. And had done several times since as Tamara adjusted to loving with a whole heart again.

"You still love him." They'd ordered salads and tea, which sat untouched in front of them. Tamara wasn't letting Mallory pay attention to such mundane things.

She did love him, of course. It wasn't news. She nodded.

"No." Tamara shook her head. "You're still *in* love with him."

She wasn't. How could she be? "He's so wrong for me. On elemental levels."

Tamara's nod wasn't encouraging at all.

And she'd yet to tell her friend about the baby she might have conceived with Braden's sperm. Or about her plan to conceive at all. She hadn't needed Tamara's help on that decision.

Which had been one of the things that had told her so clearly that she was ready. It wouldn't be easy. She wasn't kidding herself. She knew her road ahead as a working single mother, one who'd lost a child and would forever carry the fear of losing another, would be tough. She also knew it was right for her.

And that she was ready.

The fact that she'd let Bray talk her into using his sperm, she was a little less comfortable telling Tamara about that…felt a bit more defensive about doing so…

"I think maybe I've been using him as a crutch all these years," she said. "I never really gave him up, in terms of my personal security. I didn't have to worry about being alone in times of trouble because he'd always have my back."

"And that's going to change when he moves to L.A.? You think he's suddenly going to desert you?"

"No. It's just… I don't know what it is. This sad, sick feeling inside, that's what it is. And I can't figure out why it's there. What it means."

She picked up her fork and Tamara followed suit. They ate a few bites and drank tea like they were just two friends out for lunch. Except that there was silence between them.

"He's been dating other women for years, so I know it's not that I'm worried that he's starting a new life," she finally said. "He did that long ago."

"You said once that you don't know why he bothers telling you that he's going out with someone because it's not going to last."

That was true.

"So his dating isn't really moving on and starting a life without you, is it? It's just living his own life with you in it."

"But this move to L.A. is moving on to a life without me. I won't have any part in it." She'd known that already but she hated saying the words.

"Sounds that way." Tamara was watching her, her food apparently forgotten.

"And that makes me incredibly sad."

"Maybe because you're still in love with him."

She didn't want that to be true. Didn't think it was. She needed a man who could support her when she showed some emotion other than passion.

One who didn't make her feel ashamed when she burst into tears or got all excited about something.

Like she knew she would when she finally heard that she was pregnant again. Once she got over the initial spate of anxiety.

The thought struck her in the heart. She didn't want to know for sure if she was pregnant because then there'd be something to lose.

Fear was an insidious beast. It had snuck up without her knowing. And being with Tamara, her free zone where whatever thoughts she had were safe, had let her see something she'd been trying so desperately to avoid…as much as she wanted the baby, was willing to go it alone, she was scared to death, too.

"It's not a crime, you know," her friend said, bringing her back to their current conversation about Braden and still being in love with him.

Which she was not.

But she was afraid to take that pregnancy test. Maybe as much as she was excited to do so. And not just because she might be disappointed with a negative response—though there was definitely that, too.

She was a cesspool of emotion. It was a good thing Braden was out of town.

Her expression must have been giving away some of her thoughts because Tamara spoke up.

"If you're in love with him, you are. It's nothing to feel badly about," she said.

"I'm not still in love with him. We've hurt each other too much. It's there between us—this mistrust of each other in an emotional sense. I trust him to die for me, but not to hold me if I cry."

"Has he ever?"

She thought back through her memories.

"When we were first married, he used to hold me when we watched sad movies and I started to cry. It wasn't a big deal. He never said a word. He'd just move closer and hold me."

Where had that man gone? And when?

Before Tucker died, she knew that for sure. It wasn't just their son's death that had come between them. Losing Tucker had been the trigger, but things had already been coming apart.

Why hadn't she known that?

"I let him down, too," she said now. "He doesn't trust me to meet his needs in the moment, or in a relationship sense."

Not just sexually, but in other things. He wanted to come first.

It wasn't an unnatural desire.

She just hadn't been good at putting two people first. In fact, she'd sucked at it. Strange, because she tended to thirty kids in any given hour and made them all feel special.

"Besides, he's too unemotional, you know that," she said now. And she knew why. Understood why. Growing up as he did, the only male in the house with two drama queens—his mother and sister—had forced him to be the practical one at all times.

She didn't blame him.

She just wasn't good for him. Or he for her. She was truly more at peace, less stressed, when she didn't have to worry about his reactions. And she knew it was the same for him.

Which was why their friendship had such clear boundaries.

"And yet," Tamara said, "his moving leaves you with incredible sadness."

She couldn't explain it. Or lie about it, either. Which meant she had to deal with it. Tamara wouldn't let her hide or kid herself or pretend.

Stabbing lettuce with her fork, she bowed her head.

* * *

Braden called twice while she was out to lunch. Having already taken a longer break than normal, Mallory didn't take the time to call him right back. She threw herself into caring for the children, playing with them, watching over them, evaluating and helping her teachers wherever she could. She did what she did and she did it well.

Braden hadn't left a message. There was no emergency. He was probably calling to tell her his offer had been accepted. She wasn't ready to hear the news. Didn't trust herself to sound happy about it. She truly wanted him to get on with his life, because she wanted him to be happy. He was a good man, always giving of himself where he could, reliable to the core, conscientious and tending to those in his world—tenants included. He deserved to be happy.

By his definition, being happy meant being busy doing what he was driven to do.

So, yes, he needed to get on with his life.

And she needed to take her pregnancy test. If she wasn't pregnant, she wanted to get another appointment scheduled as soon as possible. So, thinking, she didn't even stop at the end of her drive to check her mail when she got home. After heading straight into the garage, she let herself in through the kitchen, dropped her bag on the counter and without bothering to turn on lights made her way to the bathroom in her master suite. The test was on the counter where she'd left it after the morning's mental debate, waiting for her.

She read the box first, then opened it and read the pamphlet inside. It had been five years since she'd done a home pregnancy test. Not much had changed.

The one difference was this test would show her

how many weeks it had been since conception with 90 percent accuracy. She didn't need that information as she knew conception and time, down to the minute. If she'd conceived.

But she could at least vouch for the test's accuracy. Maybe.

Or be more certain that it wasn't a false positive if it also got the conception right. Right?

She had to quit vacillating on when to take the damned test. She had to get on with her life.

Make it what she wanted and needed.

Stalling was done. And in less than thirty seconds so was the test. She'd waited all day to do it, and now the wait for results seemed to take a year. Weak in the knees she sat on the closed commode, picked up her phone and returned Braden's call.

His news would distract her. Put things in perspective.

It wasn't like this was her only shot to have a baby. A no answer just meant she'd have to wait another month.

He didn't pick up.

And she wasn't pregnant.

As soon as Braden could excuse himself from his business dinner at his hotel with a couple of key investors, he took the elevator straight up to his suite and called Mallory.

Was she pregnant? He was expecting a yes. They'd had no trouble getting pregnant the first time. To him the conception part was a given. How she felt about it was the question. Now that it was happening, was she sure she could handle it?

Or was she worrying already about the future fate of her unborn child?

And if she was, what could he do about it?

She picked up on the fourth ring. "The test was negative, which was to be expected," she said in lieu of hello. "I'll call the clinic in the morning and schedule the next procedure."

She said it like she was discussing having the carpets cleaned.

"I'm sorry." He was, for her. And sorry for the relief he felt, too.

"They said to expect up to six months for it to take," she reminded him.

"You're taking it well." Why that surprised him, he wasn't sure. Other than Tucker's death, Mallory had always taken life in stride. It came from growing up in foster care, he'd figured.

"It's a process," she told him. "I knew that going in. I've had all the tests. There's no reason to believe I won't conceive."

"Still... I'm sure you were hoping the baby was already on its way." Why was he doing this? Trying to get emotion out of her when she knew it was exactly what he didn't want and, therefore, would withhold it from him?

"Of course I'd hoped, but I didn't get all worked up about it. I knew the chances were good it would take more than one try."

Walking over to his bar, he pulled out a shot bottle of expensive scotch, emptied some into a glass and took a small sip.

"My offer was accepted."

"Oh, Bray! I'm glad." The sincerity in her tone warmed him. The scotch probably helped, too. "So did you get your permits going?"

"Yes." He took a couple of minutes to tell her about

the meetings he'd had. Which was more than they usually did—other than by general mention. But then, this wasn't normal—him in L.A. starting a new venture and her in San Diego trying to have a baby without him.

He took another sip and then he launched into another topic.

"I have something to discuss with you. An opportunity," he said, wandering over to the window with his glass in hand, staring out at the lights of L.A. in the distance.

"What kind of opportunity?"

"I told you I'm intending to make this L.A. project as much a replica of Braden Property Management as possible."

"Yeah." He couldn't tell by her tone if she was focused or distracted. He reminded himself she'd just suffered what had to be a crushing disappointment. No matter what she said. He knew how badly she thought she wanted another baby.

And he hoped she was distracted enough to politely decline the offer he was about to make.

"One of the things that helped make us such an instant success was our ability to offer tenants in-house daycare at a reduced rate."

He couldn't judge her reaction from her silence, but that was all she gave him.

"Since the idea was yours, and because The Bouncing Ball plays a part in the success of Braden Property Management, I'd like to know if you'd be interested in expanding, if you'd like to open a second daycare, here in L.A."

"I…"

She stopped, as if she was thinking it through. He tried to wait her out but couldn't.

"You don't have to give me an answer right now. Just think about it, would you?"

He wanted an immediate no, not more time to fret about the ramifications of the plan.

"I don't need to think about it," she said. "Of course, I'll need time to get plans in place, but I can tell you right now that I'd be honored to be a part of the L.A. venture, Braden. Thank you."

His heart sank.

Chapter Nine

Was she nuts? She couldn't be a single mother and run two businesses.

What in the heck had she been thinking? *I'd be honored to be a part of the L.A. venture, Braden. Thank you.*

Had those words really come from her mouth?

Without a moment's hesitation?

Mallory passed through the next couple of days in a blur. She made her next appointment at the Elliott Clinic in Marie Cove, assuming she ovulated as expected, and then didn't let herself think about not having another baby. It wasn't a matter of if, it was merely a matter of when.

Instead, she lay in bed Sunday night and scared herself into wondering if she was really capable of letting Braden move on without her, being his friend and supporting him while he did it. Why else would she have told him she'd be a part of his new venture?

She had absolutely no desire to own an empire. Or to live in L.A. Those were Bray's dreams, though the whole L.A. thing was new even for him.

Yet she'd jumped at the chance to join him. All weekend long she'd been reeling with the facts. He'd called once, asked her to lunch to discuss business, but she'd made an excuse, and he hadn't pushed.

Was he having second thoughts, too?

Were they back to him going and her being no part of his new life?

That thought brought back the incredible sadness she had felt at the mention of his moving.

The thought of opening a second daycare that far away brought panic. And no less desire to have her baby and get on with her life, either.

So what gave?

What was driving her?

Years of counseling and taking accountability for her own emotional health made her seek out the elusive answers.

Was she really in love with Braden still, as Tamara had said?

She had to ask.

And the answer was still the same. There was a bond there, of course. They'd been in love, had a child together and lost that child. But she didn't think she was in love with him. Anytime she tried to get there she arrived right where they'd ended—at complete odds with each other, letting each other down emotionally.

She still felt ashamed at how wild she'd been in his arms at the same time her son had died.

Still hated that she'd been away from home.

After four years it was a pretty good bet that those feelings weren't going to go away.

As night gave way to day, she got up, showered, got herself to work and greeted her children. Her days were about them, fully and completely. And yet, on Monday she was stopped in her tracks by an expression on the precious face of one of her four-year-olds. Liam was precocious and about as happy as a little boy could be. He'd come up and offered her a picture he'd drawn of a heart and told her he loved her.

She could barely hold back her tears but she pulled it off for Liam. She hid her emotion in the hug she gave him, telling him she loved him, too, and escaped as quickly as she could.

Did Braden ever think about what Tucker would be like if he'd lived? Did he ever see a four-year-old boy and wonder if Tucker would have been like him?

Her thoughts from the night before were there again, in the middle of her day. She had to tell Braden she couldn't accept his L.A. offer. She had to let him go.

She took a couple of minutes locked in her private bathroom to let the tears flow.

After having a weekend to think about it, Braden was looking forward to the idea of Mallory's daycare in L.A. He couldn't envision how it would work exactly, but he had a few ideas to run by her, ways she could manage her business, expand her business and have the life she wanted, as well. By Monday he was congratulating himself on coming up with the idea. The Bouncing Ball supported her comfortably, but with a baby to raise, the added security of a second business would further cultivate her emotional health.

Though there might be more on her plate on a day-to-day basis, at least at first, she'd have less to worry about in the big picture.

Mal had always been a big-picture girl. He'd been all about making the moment count. She'd been on the forever plan.

She didn't have time to meet him for lunch on Monday, either, and because he was leaving Tuesday morning to head back to L.A., he waited for her after work. Nothing overt; he just watched from his window for her to be heading out to her car and then called her and asked her to wait a second.

She said she had to get home to return calls she'd promised would be made that day, but when he pushed, telling her he was heading out in the morning, she relented.

If he didn't know better, he'd think she was avoiding him.

He shook his head at the thought. That was his sister's way of thinking, not his. She built a mountain of drama out of putting imaginary negative thoughts about herself in other people's heads. Mallory had no reason to avoid him. They'd established that neither of them had to worry about speaking with the other ever again.

No more hurt feelings or tense silences between them.

They weren't married anymore. They couldn't disapprove of each other's plans, thoughts, wants or desires. It had been established the day they'd divorced. Right along with the fact that they'd always be friends and have each other's backs. Or some such thing. He couldn't remember the exact words that had been said, but the understanding had been there. They had three years of proof to substantiate it.

She was sitting in her car when he got downstairs.

"Follow me home," he suggested. His place, a luxurious high-rise condo, was only a few blocks away.

When she looked ready to argue, he said, "I'll order dinner delivered and you can be home making your calls within the hour."

He was pushing too hard. But they were building their future here—futures apart from each other, while still offering friendship and support. He needed every detail laid out.

He needed this to work.

He'd been living in limbo too long and was beginning to feel like he was wasting his life.

If it was just a feeling, he'd move on. Braden tried never to build plans on something as unreliable as feelings. But when it was feeling and fact combined, he knew to push.

In her jeans and polo shirt, with her dark hair swirling around her face and shoulders, Mallory looked tired as she preceded him through his front door. And hot as hell, too. Braden liked women and got turned on as easily as the next guy. But Mallory pushed a button in him no other woman seemed to know how to push.

Probably because he had to get her out of the way before another woman could find her way in.

You'd think her continued physical rejections during the last year of their marriage, including a show of out-and-out aversion to him touching her, would have done it.

You'd think. But it hadn't.

He'd called in an order of lasagna and salad from the wine bar on the bottom floor of his building and it arrived right behind them. Mallory was looking around the condo as though something might have changed since she'd last been there three years ago, shortly after he'd moved in. She should know him better than that. She was the one into aesthetics. He liked his surroundings nice and clean, and then he just lived in them—used them for their purpose, took them for granted.

With Mallory, her surroundings were almost like a living entity, a partner in her life. She tended to them on a regular basis, changing things up, adding stuff.

He used to look around when he got home from a trip, testing himself to see if he could figure out what she'd changed while he'd been gone.

She'd challenge him and if he could work out whatever it was, he'd get sex before dinner rather than afterward.

He'd almost always had the appetizer sex.

"You want a glass of wine?" he asked, pulling the bottle he'd ordered out of the bag. He had to get his head in the game.

And get her out of his head.

"Tea's good, if you have some."

Of course he had tea. It had always been a staple for both of them. He poured a glass for her, added ice, then opened the wine for himself.

She found plates and silverware, took them to the table in the dining room, in front of French doors that led out to a balcony facing the ocean in the distance.

She'd loved the view the moment she'd seen the place. He'd known she would.

"We could have just gone to a restaurant," she said as they sat down. She hadn't looked at him since they'd been inside.

"It would have taken twice as long and you're in a hurry. Besides, we can get through more business if we aren't constantly being interrupted by wait staff."

He'd wanted their talk to be private. What they were doing, her having a baby with his sperm, that was about as private as it could get. And now, they were about to enter into a second business agreement.

"I thought maybe you wanted to show me things," she said. "You know, where things were in case you needed me to tend to them in your absence."

That was logical, he thought, since he'd given her the key.

"Like maybe how the thermostat works or where the water shut-off valve is," she continued.

Good points, both of them. "I'll do both before you leave," he said, digging into his lasagna. She'd served herself a big bowl of salad with a small slice of the lasagna, forgoing the garlic bread.

"We should have been doing this all along," he told her, at ease with her in a way he hadn't been sitting across from her at their various restaurant haunts.

At least, he felt at ease until he met her gaze across the table and all the blood in his body surged to his penis.

For a second there he froze. Did she know? What was she thinking?

No, she couldn't possibly know. His pelvis was under the table, out of her view. And far hungrier than his stomach. Lasagna wasn't what he wanted.

"I wanted to talk to you about the daycare in L.A." Mallory stabbed the lettuce delicately, chewed, then took a sip of tea.

The daycare. It was what he'd been trying to talk to her about.

It was the purpose of the meeting, he reminded himself. Not taking her to bed.

Restaurants didn't have his bed just down the hall.

Was that why they met in them?

"You know, in your new complex," she said, fork suspended as she frowned at him.

He nodded and wiped his mouth with his napkin. "That's the purpose of this meeting," he said, attacking his lasagna with a vengeance. "I have several ideas that I think might give you a lot of added security for your future, you know, with a child, and yet wouldn't run you ragged, trying to keep up with it all."

Barely giving himself time to chew and swallow, he suggested that they use The Bouncing Ball name, set it up with the same room configurations and colors, use all of the same philosophies and paperwork, apply one accounting system that would be run online to keep both facilities connected in real time, but hire a manager to run the L.A. branch.

"You could install cameras, like the ones people put in their homes to be able to see what's going on inside when they aren't home," he continued while she silently ate her salad and then finished her piece of lasagna—all four bites of it.

"That way you can monitor what's going on in every room, all day if you want to, to make certain that the children are being treated with the loving discipline that has earned you so much respect."

She wasn't really nodding, but he could tell by the expression on her face that she was interested.

"And to make certain that the philosophy stays solid, you could offer the management position to Julia, maybe. You said since John died she's been fading. Maybe a change would be good for her."

Julia, Mallory's second-in-command, had lost her husband to a motorcycle crash the year before. They were in their forties and had never been able to conceive children. Rather than adopting, Julia had chosen to work in the childcare field. She'd applied to work with Mallory before The Bouncing Ball had even opened.

"She's actually just started seeing someone," Mallory told him. "A single dad with two kids, a boy and a girl, both under ten."

"Someone from The Bouncing Ball?"

"No. She met him through a friend of a friend. He's an engineer."

He should have known that. Why hadn't he known that? It wasn't like he and Mal didn't talk regularly.

With a shrug, he took another bite of food. And then said, "So maybe Donna or someone else would be up for the move," he said, making a mental run-through of her remaining eight employees and what he knew about their qualifications and living situations.

Mallory reached her fork over toward his lasagna and they both stopped moving, staring at each other.

Eating off each other's plates had been common once upon a time. Mostly him finishing up whatever she'd left. But not once in the last few years had either of them crossed that boundary.

"I'm sorry," she said, putting her empty fork down beside her plate.

"No," he pushed his plate toward her. "Please. I'm not going to finish."

She looked at him for a few seconds. He held her gaze. He kept telling himself he should look away, that staring into her eyes was only stirring his penis even further, but he couldn't turn away. Eventually she picked up her fork and helped herself to a bite from his plate. Watching her put it into her mouth, he dropped his napkin in his lap.

It was a good thing he was moving to L.A.

A damned good thing.

Chapter Ten

She had to tell Braden that she wasn't going to open a second daycare. All that week and into the next, Mallory told herself that she'd make the call tomorrow. Each day, it would happen tomorrow.

She had to distance herself from him. They'd proven that they weren't good for each other as more than friends. After Tucker's death the ashes of their marriage had almost destroyed her.

They were just too different in the basic way they approached life. They needed different things to make them happy.

So why hadn't she stopped his talk at his condo the week before? Told him that she'd changed her mind about joining his L.A. venture?

She didn't know, really.

It wasn't like he had to know right away, she'd told herself. He'd still do the daycare with or without her.

Any work she'd need to be involved with wouldn't come about for months.

But he should know.

Driving into Marie Cove for her appointment at the clinic, exactly one month after she'd made the same drive with Braden, she settled into the rhythm of the road, wrapped in the protective silence of her car, and let her mind relax. To relive recent business with Braden step by step. She thought back to the time he called her to ask her to wait for him. No, wait, she skipped backward to when she'd avoided his attempts to meet up.

Because she'd known she needed to tell him.

Then, that Monday night, a week and a half before, he'd asked her to his condo. She hadn't even argued. Because it had made sense, with her watching over the place for him, she should probably acquaint herself with it, learn its unique foibles.

She'd been planning to take the opportunity to tell him that he'd be doing the L.A. thing without her. She'd actually been ready to do so. Having played around with the idea, she knew that it wasn't right for her.

And then he'd sat down with her, the two of them alone at the table, with that view, in his place, and he'd started talking about the daycare. And she had kept quiet.

He'd given it so much thought. Pointed out that the added security would give her extra peace of mind as she set out into single parenthood.

He'd made sense.

He'd been supporting her in her new life.

And then he'd looked at her...more than once.

Did he know that his blue eyes darkened when he was turned on? Had she ever told him?

She'd seen that look from him thousands of times

before. Had recognized it with a shock that sent ripples through her entire system.

And for a second there, she'd received an answering call from places within her she'd thought dead and gone. At least where he was concerned.

And that was why she hadn't told him she'd changed her mind.

Shaking with the truth, Mallory missed her turnoff.

Though he'd been in San Diego twice since he'd had Mallory in his condo, Braden hadn't seen her. Purposely. He needed time to get himself under control, to be mentally prepared against flashbacks before he saw her again.

He'd met a woman in L.A., an architect colleague of Don Miller, who'd done the drawings for San Diego and was already modifying them to fit the L.A. property. Don had called Anna in for consultation on a couple of points having to do with building around the natural landscaping that they'd like to keep if they could. The three of them had had lunch.

Braden had since had dinner with her. Twice.

He liked her. A lot. More than any other woman he'd dated in the past three years.

Business-minded like him, she lived alone, visited her family in San Francisco enough to be diligent and had a beautiful smile. She laughed often. And she didn't appear to have a dramatic bone in her body. From the signals she was sending, he was pretty clear that she liked him a lot, too.

He'd made a date to have lunch with her on Thursday, a week and a half after his dinner with Mallory, but had been toying with the idea of canceling all morning. When he'd spoken with his ex-wife the night before she'd mentioned her second clinic visit, scheduled for eleven that morning. She'd had a positive ovulation test.

He'd yet to tell Anna about Mallory, other than to say he was divorced and he and his ex had remained friends. The rest was left to be shared with someone when he took their relationship to the next level.

In his hotel "office," going over the final drawings to be turned over that day to the contractor, he figured he and Anna might be headed to that next level in the very near future.

But he still figured he should cancel lunch.

Mallory would be in Marie Cove.

He could text her to meet him for a quick bite by the clinic. She'd need to get back; she never liked to take time off during the day, though, as the boss, she was free to do so. Regardless, she'd need a meal.

And he needed to tell her about Anna. He could be there and back before his next appointment.

Picking up his phone, he sent the text.

Sitting alone on the table in a paper gown, with a blanket wrapped around her to ward off the chills she'd suddenly developed, Mallory waited for her doctor. Phone in hand, she tried to distract herself with one of her favorite puzzle games.

She'd been weighed, had her blood pressure checked, peed in the cup, and all that was left was the few minutes it would take for the injection of Braden's sperm into her uterus.

It was all procedure. She'd been through it before. And she didn't have a single doubt that she was doing the right thing.

What bothered her far more was the fact that she'd

failed to distance herself from Bray in the daycare venture. Because she'd been attracted to him?

It had come and gone so quickly she'd closed her mind to the possibility instantly. But she'd worried about it ever since.

She'd been turned on by her ex-husband.

Looking back, she thought maybe she was imagining the whole thing. Maybe she'd just reacted so strongly because she'd been shocked that he'd been turned on. Shocked to see that look in his eye. Or maybe she was hormonal, her body raging with the need to be a mother again.

Maybe it was because she was using his sperm.

Her phone vibrated with a text. The message flashed up on her screen.

Meet me for a quick bite?

The timing was no mistake. She was certain of that.

Yes.

She was going to tell him she was out of the L.A. deal.

"Mallory? You can get dressed," Dr. Sharon Miller said as she came into the exam room and closed the door.

Last time a nurse had come in before the doctor with a tray filled with procedural materials. She'd been expecting the nurse first.

"Get dressed? I don't understand."

Surely she didn't have the wrong time. They'd checked her in like they were expecting her. Put her through the pre-insemination rigmarole.

Dr. Miller's smile threw her off a bit. And then she heard, "You're pregnant!"

Everything inside her stopped and then restarted in double speed. Her heart pounded. Her breathing quickened. Her stomach jumped. It was like she could feel everything individually. In slow motion.

"I…"

She didn't know what to say. Was afraid to believe it.

"Your urine test came back positive. That's why, once we've started the monthly injections, we always check."

"But I had a period." A light one. Really light. But that wasn't all that unusual for her when she was stressed.

Putting a hand on Mallory's, Dr. Miller said, "You're pregnant, sweetie."

She was pregnant? As in…right then, right there, inside her, she had a new baby? She wasn't just Mallory Harris, divorced mother of a deceased child anymore?

She was an expectant mother?

"I ovulated," she said through a dry throat, swallowing to try to fix that malady.

"An ovulation test will commonly show up positive if you're pregnant."

She hadn't known that.

"I'm pregnant?"

"Four weeks," Dr. Miller was still smiling. "That's one benefit to insemination—no guessing as to gestation timing."

Mallory sat there in her gown, the blanket wrapped around her, hugging her stomach, and nodded.

"You'll need to see your OB as soon as possible," the doctor continued, talking about vitamins, prenatal care, the rounds of tests she'd be going through. Most of which she'd done with Tucker, too. "I'm recommending that they do a six-week ultrasound," she said. "It's common with fertility and insemination procedures, just to make certain that everything is okay."

She added Mallory's projected due date: December 10th. And then said, "I'll leave you to get dressed. It was nice meeting you, Mallory. Good luck and Merry Christmas!"

The woman was out the door and Mallory sat there with her mouth hanging open.

Merry Christmas! Last Christmas she'd been on a boat with friends, feeling more alone than she'd ever felt in her life.

By next Christmas she was going to be a family again. A mother. With her own baby to hold. Assuming everything was okay.

I'm recommending that they do a six-week ultrasound...just to make certain that everything is okay.

As she remembered Dr. Miller's words, fear struck. Instantaneous and sharp.

Assuming all went well with that, she'd have to get past the five-month mark before she'd really be home free.

No. Shaking her head, she slid to her feet, reaching for her clothes with shaking hands. She wasn't going to let fear rule her life. Her past would not steal from her future.

She was going to be a mother again! That was this moment's truth.

Her mind would remain firmly on what was, not on what could be.

She would control her fear.

Reality was she had a baby growing inside her!

Holy crap!

* * *

The Elliott Clinic was not far off the freeway. Using his GPS to find a nearby place for a quick lunch, he'd texted Mallory with the address. She was already there when he arrived. Already seated among a far wall of booths, all filled with well-dressed, mostly business-looking patrons. The two men right behind her seemed to be in serious discussion.

Just as he'd been the day before when he'd met with his top investor.

At the moment, he envied those two men. He'd much rather be talking money than telling his ex-wife that he was dating again. If he and Anna did hook up on a more serious basis, he'd need to make certain that he didn't have to dread an emotional conversation like the one that could be potentially ahead.

Him dating wasn't that big of a deal. He'd told Mallory half a dozen times about going out with various different women.

But Anna was different.

She was L.A. The start of his new life.

At least that's how he feared Mallory was going to see it. She'd make a bigger deal of it than it was at the moment.

She'd ask him if her suspicions were true.

And he wouldn't be able to deny them, because, at some point in the future, they might be.

She'd already ordered their tea. It was sitting on the table as he slid into his side of the booth. Not able to meet her eyes, his gaze dropped to the table and met her breasts just above it. They looked fabulous in a purple shirt. Just fabulous.

"I ordered you a grilled chicken sandwich with sweet

potato fries," she told him. "Sorry, but I need to get back."

"No, that's great." Lifting his gaze, he smiled at her. She looked radiant and for a second his penis came more fully to life. Was she that happy to see him?

Then he caught himself.

She'd just been inseminated again, so of course she looked radiant.

What was with all of his overreaction around this woman? Was her emotional approach to life contagious? Something he'd caught when they'd been married, like some disease he couldn't shake?

It had been three years, and now he'd suddenly had a relapse?

"Look, I know we don't have much time, so I just need to tell you right away. I can't do the L.A. daycare thing, Braden. I appreciate the offer so much. And you're right, it could be a great thing, but I've decided to pass on your offer."

Everything settled inside him. He was calm. Analytical. Himself again.

"Why? Other than the initial investment for startup, which I told you I'd loan you at today's rate minus a percent due to the fact that I stand to benefit from the deal, this won't be a drain on you. Especially if you let someone else manage the place for you, with cameras installed so you don't keep feeling like you have to run up and check on things. And it will ensure your future security."

He thought it had all been worked out. The idea made sense. He was going to do the daycare. The business plan had already shown itself highly successful in San Diego. Someone was going to benefit. Might as well be someone he cared about.

"Besides, with your philosophies, your hiring of employees, your oversight, I know that the daycare will be the asset I need it to be so my future tenants feel comfortable leaving their kids there. And you have no problem offering the lower rates for tenants because you've already seen how, in the end, you benefit financially from the built-in clients.

"Added to that, we've got the success of The Bouncing Ball in San Diego to show them. Prospective tenants who would be daycare clients can drive down and visit you there to see the great environment you have to offer them."

He might have kept right on talking if their food hadn't been delivered.

She'd ordered half a grilled chicken sandwich with a cup of soup and dug right in.

"So?" he asked after he'd taken the edge off with a couple of bites.

She shook her head. "It sounds good, Bray, but I can't."

The woman wasn't budging. Studying her, he didn't get it.

Which was probably why they were divorced.

He wanted her to get it.

He wanted her to be part of the L.A. venture. It made practical, financial sense.

She'd be taken care of. And he could move on more easily.

"I'll be there to check on things," he told her. "You know I wouldn't let anything untoward happen. I've got your back. I always have."

Her smile made him hungry for sex again.

"I know, and that's why I can't do it."

Throwing a hand up he said, "I don't get it."

"The whole point of your move to L.A. was to start your own life. To move on. We both know that means moving on from me. From us. How are you going to do that if I follow along with you?"

"I'll have an entirely new life in L.A. Living in a new place, hanging out with new people." Like Anna. And others he'd met in the past weeks. Guys who'd invited him to play golf. A bar he'd found where there were high-stakes dart tournaments. He'd been pretty good at darts in college.

Her look had him stumped. Was it pity he saw on her face?

No, but…something.

"Answer me this. If it wasn't for the fact that we both know life was growing stagnant and had to change, that we needed a break between us…if this was just a business venture, would you accept the offer?"

"Probably. As you said, it makes sense in a lot of ways."

"So let's table this for now, okay? Think about it some more. See how it goes with me in L.A. and you in San Diego. I think you'll see that the distance we need will be there."

She shook her head. "I know I need to say no, Bray."

"Please," he pushed. Because he couldn't not. The plan made perfect sense for both of them. And then something occurred to him. She'd had to fight hard to recover from the panic attacks and fear that had beset her in the early days after Tucker's death. They'd only lasted a month or two, but the fact that they'd happened at all had scared her. "Are you afraid you can't let go of me?"

Her gaze shot up. He got hot again.

"I'm pregnant, Bray."

He dropped his sandwich. At first he didn't even notice. All he could see was the glow in her eyes, that odd look again. It wasn't pity. It was compassion. Her "mother" look, he'd once dubbed it. He should have known.

"But you said you had your—"

"I did. But they did a test this morning and it turns out I'm pregnant."

Hmm.

Well.

Whoa.

He nodded a bit.

And when he thought maybe he had assimilated the situation he said, "I'm seeing someone."

Chapter Eleven

That first weekend Mallory was consumed with baby buying. She'd done Tucker's room in yellows and greens, giraffes, elephants and monkeys. This time around she chose primary colors, balloons and bears, mostly. And she bought a new crib—she'd gotten rid of Tucker's the day he'd been taken from it—in a new style, too; instead of brown, white this time with a changing table to match. She filled her car and went back a second time, filling it again.

If you build it, they will come. The phrase came to her from somewhere in her past. From a movie about baseball fields. She couldn't remember when she'd seen it or with whom, but since the words presented themselves out of the blue, she took them to heart.

She'd build the nursery and her baby would come.

And then she was done.

There'd be more to add as the months passed. Outfits, diapers, cute things she'd pick up for the room as she saw them. And a rocker—she was thinking old-fashioned this time, not the glider kind she'd had before. But, for the most part, what had taken her months the first time around was done in three days.

No researching was necessary this time. She knew what kind of swing she preferred and why; she had them at the daycare. Car seat, portable crib, bouncy seat and high chair, too. She was a woman who knew pretty much everything about baby paraphernalia—down to the style of breast pump.

By Sunday afternoon she was satisfied with how the room across the hall from hers looked. Liked how the portable crib fit into her room's decor.

And then she panicked. What if something happened? What if she miscarried? Should she have waited until she'd passed the critical three-month stage? What if she'd jinxed things? Like she'd left Tucker that night?

If you build it, they will come.

She wasn't jinxing; she was building.

Heart pounding, she concentrated on slowing her air intake so she didn't hyperventilate. She drew in deeper breaths as she thanked God that Braden wasn't around to witness her weekend.

Then she called Tamara.

Having driven to San Diego on Saturday to retrieve his boat and dock her in her new home not far from the hotel where he was staying, Braden took Anna out on the water Sunday. She wasn't into fishing—or sunbathing, either, for that matter. But she had a great time captaining the boat when he offered her the wheel, laughing when she hit a wake. Right behind her, his arms wrapping her as he taught her, he laughed, too.

And he told himself that this was living.

But later that afternoon, when they docked and she made it clear that she was open to them spending the rest of the day—and the night—together, he chose to get back to work. He had meetings in the morning—Braden Property Management business, not new build business—and needed to prepare.

Mallory was pregnant. It was right that he let Anna know before he had sex with her. Just in case she had a problem with it.

He didn't expect she would. Didn't see why she would.

Still, with Mallory's news still so fresh, he was pretty certain the decent thing was to let Anna know.

He called Mal on the way back to his hotel, figuring he'd get her opinion on the matter. She was a woman. She'd probably know better than he how to present their situation to his potential girlfriend. She didn't pick up.

Out baby shopping, he was sure. Ever since she'd told him she was expecting again, he was remembering how she'd been the first time, so he was certain he could predict her actions, even down to the stores she'd visit. It would take months. She'd think of nothing else outside of work.

At first, he'd been as bad as she was. The memory creeped in as he pulled into the underground parking garage and took the elevator up to his suite. He'd heard of an out-of-the-way spot that sold handmade nursery furniture and he'd called Mallory, convincing her to go with him to see if they could get the crib she wanted.

He'd been willing to play hooky but she'd made them wait until Saturday.

They'd painted the nursery together. He'd accidentally bumped into her with the roller. She'd given him such a saucy look he'd slid it up her shirt. And then dropped it. And his pants. About as quickly as she'd dropped hers.

Lovemaking had always been like that with them. Spontaneous. Intense. All the time.

Until she'd started to pull back. He'd understood. It had been getting harder and harder for her to find a comfortable position just to sit or lie down. Having him in her space, on her space, hadn't helped.

He'd told himself that after the baby was born things would return to normal.

Instead there'd been a new normal. Mallory had become a mother.

Being a wife didn't seem to interest her anymore.

Until that last night.

Maybe he'd been too impatient and hadn't given her enough time to adjust. It was the first time in her life she'd been aware of being with biological family. Of course that had to have had an effect on her.

She'd needed him to sit with her.

He'd needed her to have sex with him. Or even just sit with him.

To matter.

He couldn't blame her for how she'd felt, how motherhood had completed her. None of what she had done had been wrong. She'd been a great mom. A working mom.

And it wasn't like she hadn't still talked to Braden, asked about his day.

It hadn't just been the lack of sex, either, though.

When she'd looked at him, it had been like she wasn't really seeing him. She was seeing whatever Tucker was doing, even if he was in his crib asleep.

And when he'd talked, at least one ear had always been listening to or for the baby. She'd carried that damned monitor everywhere.

He'd started to resent the thing. Which was why he'd pushed so hard to have her to himself for one night.

It had been quite a night. The best sex ever. And

more, Mallory had seen him again. Heard him. She'd cared that he was there seeing her, loving her. He'd thought that night had solved their problems. He'd been ready to head back home to their son and give her the time she'd needed to adjust, figuring that she'd be paying more attention to him, too.

Instead, they'd gotten the call…and after that, everything just went from horrible to worse.

With a glass of whiskey in hand he stood at the window of his hotel suite, disgruntled, a sense of dissatisfaction settling over him. In his mind he returned to an earlier time. The moment he'd known that he and Mallory were heading for divorce. He'd been in a hotel similar to the current one, away on business and dreading going home.

He'd had a woman invite him to spend the night with her earlier in the evening. He hadn't done so, of course. He'd taken his marriage vows seriously and would never have cheated on Mallory, just as he'd been certain she'd never cheat on him.

But he'd been tempted. God, he'd been tempted.

Which was how he'd known.

Sipping from his glass, he dropped down to the sofa, still facing the window.

In the beginning, though, when they'd first found out they were having a baby, there'd been nothing like it.

She was experiencing that same feeling now.

While he was back in a hotel room. Planning to sleep with Anna as soon as he told her that Mallory was pregnant.

Funny how life seemed to go in circles and still got so screwed up.

The first thing Mallory told Tamara about, when the woman showed up at her door Sunday rather than just returning her call as they'd discussed, was Braden's offer for expanding The Bouncing Ball business with a second daycare in his L.A. complex.

Tamara hadn't needed to come, but Mallory understood why she had. Mallory had made similar visits to the home Tamara shared with Flint Collins and the precious little baby sister he'd inherited, and she would continue to do so whenever Tamara called her.

They were two strong women who'd suffered debilitating grief but were determined to live happy lives. They shared things that most people who'd never lost a child would ever fully understand.

"Did you tell him you'd do it?" Tamara's expectant expression settled her a bit. She could have looked worried. Or horrified.

Bringing glasses of tea out to the small patio off her kitchen, she handed one to her friend and sat down with her at the round glass table. "I told him no," she reported happily. Then she amended her response. "At first I said yes, but when I thought about it and the things we'd talked about, I knew that I was doing it for the wrong reason."

"Which was?"

"To continue to be a part of his life. I'm using him as a crutch. Preventing myself—and him—from moving on."

She had more to say. A lot more. But she wanted this part cleared up first.

Because it really mattered.

Being a mother was only part of her life. Something else she'd learned the hard way. When she'd lost Tucker, she'd lost herself. She'd had her own identity so wrapped up in his—her only known biological person in the world—that she'd almost lost her own life. Had her son lived, her being so consumed by him would not have been good for him. Though she didn't ever see herself marrying again, didn't see herself being successful at being both mother and wife, she still needed to have healthy adult relationships. For her own sake and that of her child.

"When he made the offer, I wasn't sad anymore about his plans. Which told me that I'd wanted to be a part of them."

Tamara was frowning now.

"And before you say it, don't," Mallory said. "He wasn't offering for the same reason. We aren't two people who are still in love and meant to be together." Ever since Tamara had opened up her heart and fallen in love again, she was seeing true love everywhere.

Mostly, Mallory found the characteristic endearing. Except for now, when it was turned erroneously on her.

"Braden was just being Braden. He had a whole list of reasons why joining him would be good business. Good for me financially, too."

When Tamara asked what they were, she listed them all, almost verbatim as Bray had presented them to her. "Besides," she added, "he's seeing someone again."

Tamara frowned again.

"What?" Mallory asked her.

"If he's involved, and his reasoning is sound, are you sure you aren't letting your past rob from your future?" she asked, her gaze steady.

"I'm confused." Mallory stared back. "Isn't that what I'd be doing if I accepted his offer?"

"Is it?"

She'd like to have been able to get irritable with her friend and move on. But that wasn't why she'd called Tamara.

"I don't know," she said. "I turned him down. Thursday, at lunch. He told me he was leaving the door open. He reiterated all the reasons it was a good idea. He said nothing had to be done for a few months and just wanted me to think about it."

"So are you?"

Obviously she was. She had some pretty incredible news to share, and here she was, rehashing the whole Braden thing again.

"I want to do it," she said. "I just want to make certain I'm doing it for the right reasons."

"Then take the time he's given you. Revisit it from time to time over the next couple of months. See if your feelings change."

She smiled, feeling her clarity returning. "Thank you."

"Of course." Tamara smiled back and made a crack about being glad to have the excuse to get away from cleaning out the shed. The baby, Diamond Rose, was spending the afternoon and evening with her paternal grandparents. Tamara just wanted to be home in time for bath, bottle and bedtime.

Mallory grinned. Hugely. She couldn't help it.

"I have other news," she admitted, sitting forward. "I'm pregnant."

"You're what?" Tamara squealed loudly enough for all of the neighbors to hear. Jumping up, she tilted the table and spilled tea from both of their glasses. "You're pregnant?" She stood there, hands on her hips, staring at Mallory, who nodded, still grinning inanely.

"But…who's the father?"

She didn't even hesitate as she told Tamara about her plan to have a child. The trips to the fertility clinic. The decision to use insemination.

"You've been working on this for months and never said a word?"

"I didn't need clarity," she said. "When I was ready, I just knew I was ready." She stood and Tamara grabbed her up in a nice long hug. One she'd been craving since she heard the news.

"You want to see the nursery?" she asked, taking her friend's hand and leading her back into the house, through the living room and down the hall. "It's been hard not telling you, but I wanted to wait until I was pregnant first. They said it could easily take up to six months and there was no point in anyone else wondering and waiting every month."

"Except that I would have been happy to share that with you, so you weren't going through it alone."

She hadn't been. Braden had known.

But Braden's part in the process was the one thing she hadn't shared. Nor did she share it as her friend oohed and ahhed over the nursery, lingering a bit as she touched the crib, the swing cover, causing Mallory to wonder if maybe Tamara was thinking about trying one more time to have a child of her own.

"Just don't hold out on me when the fear hits," Tamara said, standing close as she held Mallory's gaze. "You know it's going to come."

"It's already started."

"Don't go through it alone."

"I won't."

"No matter what time of day or night."

She'd answered a couple of middle-of-the-night calls from Tamara during the past months.

"I promise."

She swore she'd call her friend anytime she needed her, then answered all of Tamara's questions about the insemination process, the doctor's instructions, her due date. The one thing she still didn't do was tell her friend that Braden was her sperm donor.

Because it wasn't critical. The sperm was from a donor. She'd just chosen to use a donor whose family history she knew. For safety's sake. And one who'd offer another kind of insurance as well—a biological family for her child if anything should happen to her.

It was all just science and legalities.

She had clarity on that.

Chapter Twelve

Braden was on his second whiskey, paperwork spread out in front of him on the coffee table in his suite, staring out the window as dusk fell over the city, casting shadows on mountains in the distance, when Mallory called him back.

"Sorry. Tamara stopped over," she said, dissipating his growing sense that she really was avoiding him.

Nonsense was what that was.

But Tamara… Mention of the other woman made him tense. Mallory and Tamara didn't go shopping or to the theater like other friends. No, they only got together when one or the other of them was on the brink of an emotional meltdown.

It wasn't like he found anything wrong with that. In truth, he found it admirable. It just made him uncomfortable to the point of drinking more.

"Is she okay?" he asked because it was his duty to be polite.

"Yeah. I called her."

Oh.

"You're struggling?" *Already.* "Because of the baby?"

"No."

Oh. Well then... "I was calling to ask your opinion on something," he said, watching as lights slowly popped on in the distance, thinking it would be one hell of an onerous task to count them all.

And then he wondered what it said about him that he spent so much time paying attention to the lights outside his window.

"Of course." Mallory's reply was steady. Easy. Kind. She didn't sound like she was close to any kind of breakdown at all.

Relieved, he took a sip of whiskey and said, "I think it's only right that I tell Anna that you're pregnant, and that I am your sperm donor. I was hoping you might have some suggestion about how I do that."

"You don't do it."

"Of course I have to let her know that—"

"Braden, the whole point here is that you just donated sperm. Period. I'm not having your child. I'm having my child."

Standing, he left his glass on the table and walked over to the window. "Yeah, I wanted to talk to you about that."

"What?" A definite tone of wariness entered her voice.

"I think you should put my name on the birth certificate."

"Wait. Are you're trying to tell me that you want to be the baby's father?"

"No! Of course not!" Dear God, no. But he couldn't help wondering... Had her voice changed yet again, as though she was open to the possibility? Or had that just been incredulity at his presumptuousness? "I'm not going to renege on my agreement to support you in raising a child on your own," he quickly assured her. "But I was thinking about what you said, about knowing that I'd take the child if something ever happened to you, so that your child would have biological family other than you."

"What does that have to do with your name on the birth certificate?"

"I wouldn't have to prove paternity. The child would come to me immediately."

He didn't know if her pause was good or bad and he didn't like not knowing. He probably should have waited to have the conversation face-to-face so he'd at least have a chance at reading her expression.

"We could have papers drawn up immediately with me giving up all custodial rights to you—"

"I don't—"

"Think about it, Mal. What if down the road something happens to you and I'm not in the picture? I don't know about it and they give the kid to social services." The idea set off a maelstrom of quandary inside him.

He didn't do quandary. He found logic, made plans, acted.

"You're planning to lose contact with me?"

That wasn't what he'd said. She was doing that thing again where she read emotional impact into words that weren't at all intended to deliver a punch.

"I was thinking more along the lines of you choosing not to be in touch, for whatever reason. Or the two of us drifting apart as a mutual thing."

Another pause. How had things gotten so out of hand?

He returned to the couch and took another sip of his

second shot. He'd probably be feeling a whole lot better if it was double that.

"Look, it just occurred to me that my name on the birth certificate would give you further peace of mind," he told her. "Because you put such weight on the fact that I'd be willing to step in in case of emergency. I was just trying to make that a foregone conclusion for you. You'd never have to worry about me changing my mind or getting married and having a wife who talked me out of keeping my word to you. Which is also why I thought I should tell Anna."

"You're thinking about marrying her?" The question ended on a high note.

"No! Not anytime soon at any rate. We've only been on two dates. I just… I like her. And my point in being here in L.A. is to get on with my life. I made a promise to you that I would be a father to that child if anything happened to you. Which means that any woman who is sharing my life would have to be willing to take that on."

Or she wouldn't be sharing his life.

"If you're on the birth certificate you'd be responsible for child support."

He didn't give a damn about the money.

"We could set up a college fund."

"You can't pay for my baby's college."

"I'd have to pay if something happened to you. Consider it the alimony you wouldn't take during the divorce."

He'd offered. Many times. Pushed, even. And lost unequivocally on that point.

"Give me time to think about it, okay? I've got another eight months before the birth certificate will be an issue."

"But you'll think about it?" He dumped the rest of his glass of whiskey down the sink at the bar and grabbed a bottle of tea from the refrigerator.

"Of course. You've asked me to, so I will."

So Mallory. She'd accommodate a scorpion if it had a way of communicating its needs to her.

"And, Bray? Seriously, I'd hold off on saying anything to Anna. At least until you know that you want to marry her. This is my business, too, and I definitely don't want every woman you date to know about it. I don't want anyone to know, which was the whole point of insemination to begin with. I get your point, You're right that your wife would have a right to know about your promise to me. But can we at least wait until you know for sure you want to get married before you say anything?"

She hadn't asked him to donate his sperm. He'd pushed. The ball really was in her court.

"Fair enough."

Mallory thanked him, wished him good-night and hung up.

So did that mean he was now free to sleep with Anna?

She'd made it clear she was free that evening. And open to deepening their relationship.

Setting the tea on the table by his business papers, Braden sat down and got to work.

Other than Tamara and Braden, Mallory didn't tell anyone she was pregnant during the next two weeks. The ultrasound with her own OB in San Diego loomed and she wanted to make certain that everything was okay before she spread her news.

There'd be a lot of questions, "Who's the father?" being number one, she was sure. And, if something was awry, there'd be a lot of sympathy. She was prepared to answer the questions when the time came. She'd made a conscious choice. There would be those who didn't understand. She wouldn't hold their lack of understanding against them.

She talked to Braden a few times during those two weeks. Mostly just touching base. He'd mentioned Anna a time or two, so she knew he was still seeing the other woman. Might be a record for him, she thought.

Not that it concerned her.

And yet…she found herself obsessing about the other woman when she was too tired to control her thoughts. Who was she? Where did she come from? What did she do? What did she look like? Was she good enough for him?

Of course not. That last answer she had, unequivocally. She didn't know how she knew the answer, she just did. And she would be relieved when he called to say that it was over.

He always did.

But what if this time he didn't? He'd been staying in L.A. almost full-time. What if dating this Anna person really was him moving on with his life?

Well, she was moving on with hers, she reminded herself as she checked in for her ultrasound that third Thursday in April. At only six weeks she wasn't showing at all, nor did she have any signs of morning sickness yet, either.

She'd had it bad with Tucker, for about a week. Hadn't been able to keep anything down. Poor Bray had been so worried, standing there over the toilet with her, holding her hair back, giving her cool washcloths when she was done puking her guts out.

He'd tried. He'd really tried.

She hoped Anna got that about him. That he tried.

So what was wrong with her that trying wasn't enough? What had she expected—perfection?

"Mrs. Harris?" the technician called her name. Mallory saw no reason to correct her title to Ms. Harris was her married name.

Thinking about names got her to the hallway. Then she had little to distract her from the fact she was about to go in for a test that could show something wasn't okay.

She'd built her nursery. She was building her new life. So "they" would come, right? Her baby—he or she would have a safe little home in there.

"If we're lucky you'll be able to hear the heartbeat this morning," the technician—*Adelaide* her nametag read—told her as they entered the room. "I don't know if they told you that or not."

She shook her head as she climbed up on the table as directed.

"We can record it," Adelaide continued as she lifted Mallory's shirt high enough to completely expose her stomach and then rolled under the waistband of her jeans, as well. "That way the father can hear it, too."

Recordings weren't her concern at the moment.

And...the father?

As Adelaide spread cold gel all over her stomach, Mallory stared at the ceiling and thought about the first time she'd heard Tucker's heartbeat. It had been during her normal prenatal check. Braden had been at work and she hadn't thought to ask if he wanted to come along. Those early doctor visits, they'd felt...feminine. Between her, her doctor and her baby.

They hadn't offered to record it, either.

Braden hadn't seemed to think anything of it. He'd

been super excited to know that she'd heard it. He'd asked her how it sounded, and when she'd said it was fast, he'd looked worried, asking questions until she'd assured him that the doctor had said it was perfectly normal.

The technician put a handheld device on her belly, started moving it around.

Why hadn't she thought to invite Braden to hear Tucker's heartbeat for himself?

"Okay, you can look right here and see..." The technician's voice fell off. She adjusted the transformer, and Mallory turned her head to look at the screen.

She'd told herself she wouldn't. She'd just let them do their work and assume everything was fine. It wasn't like she'd know what she was looking at anyway. Not this early.

"See...right here," the technician said. "This is your baby."

She didn't see a baby. She saw something that looked kind of like a peanut still in the shell. A really small one. If she looked really hard at the differences in the shadows, she could almost make out a bunny head, too.

"Is there a heartbeat?"

"Not yet," the technician said, moving her apparatus around. She'd grown quiet. Her tone more business-like than chipper. Honing in on one part of Mallory's stomach, she put more gel on her and stared at the screen.

Oh, God. Everything wasn't okay.

She couldn't do this. No. It wasn't right.

She took a deep breath. She had to handle what life gave her. There simply was no other choice. Tucker had taught her that. Her sweet baby boy. He'd be in heaven, watching over her.

"There..." Frowning, Adelaide held the transformer still.

"Is that a heartbeat?" It sounded different from what

she remembered of Tucker's. Of course he'd been older. But the sound was so…jumbled. Not a regular rhythm.

There was something wrong with her baby's heart.

"It's two actually," the woman said. "I wasn't sure at first, but there are definitely two babies there."

Two babies?

But…

"Do twins run in your family?"

She had no idea. And Braden's? Did they run in his? She didn't know that, either.

But she knew she could find out.

And she would.

As soon as she got a hold of herself.

She was having two babies? Kids who'd always have each other. Who'd never know what it was to grow up alone.

Two little ones to hold. To raise. To watch grow.

Twice the love.

Lying on the table with her smeared belly exposed, Mallory burst into tears.

Chapter Thirteen

Braden was getting ready to go into a theater with Anna to see a touring Broadway production of *Hamilton*, something she particularly wanted to see, when his phone buzzed with Mallory's call.

"I'm sorry. I have to take this," he told her, leaving her to find their seats on her own while he stepped out into the lobby.

"Everything okay?" he asked. She almost never called in the evening.

"I just…was wondering…when you're going to be in San Diego."

"I can come tonight if you need me. What happened?"

"Nothing happened. I'm just calling to arrange a meal. You know, lunch or dinner, so we can talk."

Her words said one thing, her tone of voice another. His concern turned into something more.

"Is the baby okay?" He knew she couldn't handle another loss. Didn't deserve it.

"Yes."

"You're sure?"

"Positive."

Did she just chuckle?

The lights blinked, signaling that the play was ready to start. He made a quick mental review of the next day's calendar. Fridays were usually lighter than Mondays, but still booked. He'd been planning a trip home over the weekend. Had even thought about maybe inviting Anna to accompany him. But then there'd be the whole overnight thing.

He was pretty sure he wanted sex as badly as she seemed to. He just wasn't ready to take a chance on sex making them more committed than he was sure he wanted to be. Yet.

"Can you do lunch tomorrow?" he asked. And then amended, "Or dinner would be better so I could have a full day of business."

"You're going to be here tomorrow?"

Now he was.

"Yes." A couple of his meetings were over the internet. He could do those from his San Diego office. And reschedule other things.

His mind raced. Mallory only called if it was important. "You're sure everything's okay?" He hated not knowing what was going on with her. How could he stay on top of things, make certain that he was giving her the support he'd promised, if he didn't know what he was dealing with?

"I'm sure, Bray." She sounded sure.

Walking back toward the hall that led to his entry into the theater, he relaxed, made arrangements to meet his ex-wife not far from work for dinner the following evening and went in to enjoy an evening of Broadway with his girlfriend.

Life was moving on.

Just as he'd planned.

Mallory was both gleeful and scared to death as she dressed for work on Friday. Instead of her normal pants and polo shirt, she wore one of her many light cotton skirts—this one in shades of burgundy with beige flowers—a beige top and a three-quarter sleeve, lightweight maroon sweater. Her jeweled flat sandals matched perfectly and completed the comfy but feminine feel she was going for. Because she had a late parent meeting to discuss a precocious three-year-old who belonged in a four-year-old class academically, she wouldn't have time to go home and change before dinner with Braden.

It was just a normal dinner, she told herself, at a restaurant they frequented often.

Except this time they were talking about her twins.

Did he have twins in his family?

It didn't really matter; she was having them whether he did or not. But the doctor seemed to want to know. Something to do with the insemination process.

She'd been assured there was no danger to her babies, either way, but they wanted it on the record, if possible.

Her babies.

She was having twins. Of all things.

All by herself.

It stood to reason that they'd both be hungry at once, need to be changed at the same time. How would she choose who to tend to first?

Up late looking on the internet the night before, she finally nixed that endeavor. There were more horror stories and warnings, parents talking more about the challenges than anything else. She could come up with her own list of potential problems without any help, thank you.

And she was a certified child-development specialist with a college degree in the field who worked with dozens of children, not just two, every single day.

She could do this.

Arriving at the restaurant her usual fifteen minutes early, expecting to have a good ten minutes to acclimate herself to a friendly conversation minus any of the drama rambling through her, she was surprised to see Braden already there. Stepping away from the wall off to the side of the hostess's desk, he greeted her with a kiss to the cheek and, with his hand at her back, walked with her as the hostess showed them to their table.

It was a booth by a wall, with no window to look out. No ocean to see. Leaving her staring at him as she reeled from the touch of his hand at the small of her back. It had been so long since he'd touched her there. She was making too much of it, she was sure. Totally overreacting.

As was her want for more. Like a kiss full on the lips instead of the cheek. Maybe with some tongue touching.

What was wrong with her?

It had to be the pregnancy. Or, worse, perverseness because she knew he was seeing someone. She hoped to God it wasn't that. She wasn't that small, was she?

She wanted Braden happy. That's all she'd ever wanted for him.

Yeah, she'd love it if they could still be married, but they'd torn each other apart. It was much better to be friends than to lose him completely.

Glancing over, she caught him looking at her with

that darker blue shadow in his eyes. The one that told her he'd rather have sex than dinner.

Again, it had to be her misreading the look.

"I didn't really plan to be in San Diego today." His voice was soft, taunting her, though there was no way he'd know that.

Pray he never knew that. She'd be so humiliated. And he'd feel badly, as if it was his fault and as if he owed her for the fact that her body suddenly seemed to be coming alive for him again.

It *had* to be the pregnancy, and that had been totally her fault. Her choice.

"You didn't?" she asked when she could trust her voice not to crack.

He shook his head. And she wasn't sure what she was supposed to make of that.

They ordered and as they ate, Braden talked about the progress being made on the new L.A. build and the pros and cons of living in a hotel. He missed his own bed, his own bathroom and closet more than he'd thought he would.

She wondered if he missed San Diego, too, but didn't ask.

He didn't ask why she'd called the dinner meeting. Needing some time to get over her emotional reaction to seeing him, to him touching her lower back, she didn't tell him. She didn't trust herself not to gush. Or cry. And she definitely didn't want to add those flames to a relationship that seemed to be changing in spite of their desires and efforts and promises to not let that happen.

When their plates were cleared and he was paying the bill, she figured she'd ask him about his family's twin history as they were parting at their vehicles. Make it just a quick oh-by-the-way thing.

He asked her to go for a walk with him, instead. They were downtown, one block from a row of shops and hotels along the ocean. With the balmy May evening air feeling good to her heated skin and her fears right there ready to mock her, she agreed, thinking a walk with her ex-husband was better than fighting with her own mind.

Their hands brushed and she immediately stepped to the side, adjusting her walk to prevent another touch.

"I want to apologize," she said, when she'd meant to ask about the history of twins in his family.

"For what?"

"When we had Tucker I didn't even think to include you when I went to the doctor, you know, hearing the heartbeat and all that."

"I didn't ask to go."

"But you'd have gone if I'd asked, wouldn't you?"

"Of course."

"I've been thinking about it all day." The words poured out even though she'd promised herself she wouldn't do this to him. Wouldn't drag him back into the emotional quagmire he detested. "I wasn't fair to you, Bray. I excluded you from things that maybe you didn't necessarily care about or think were a big deal, but if you'd been there…well, maybe they could have been."

"You were having a baby. I wasn't. Of course there were things only you got to experience."

"But I didn't even try to make you a part of them." And after Tucker was born, she'd never once asked him to rise in the night to get the baby. She'd been breast-feeding, so she'd had to get up anyway. Besides, he'd been working while she'd taken four months off.

"We painted the nursery together," he said, and out of the blue she was suffused with heat again. She'd forgotten about that and how that venture had been interrupted with sex on the floor of the nursery.

Her nipples tingled and liquid pooled below. *Hormones, all hormones*, she assured herself. With a little dab of memory mixed in.

"I just… I'm sorry I robbed you of the chance to fully experience the birth of your first child."

There. She'd said it.

And she felt better. Sort of. She could never give those experiences back to him.

"I missed you." Hands in his pockets, he stared ahead of them.

"What, this week?" she asked. "We talked twice." But she knew that wasn't what he'd meant. He was wearing the purple tie, and she wondered if he'd chosen her favorite color because he'd known he was having dinner with her.

Like she'd chosen her outfit for him.

"Back then. It wasn't so much that I couldn't experience everything you were experiencing. It was that you didn't seem to need me around."

She felt as though she'd been softly and kindly slapped. If such a thing could happen.

Truth was, she hadn't needed him, not in the way she should have. She'd been deeply in love with him, hadn't wanted to lose him. But on a day-to-day basis, she'd been in heaven those months she'd been a mom—before and after Tucker's birth.

"I don't know how to be all in with two different people," she told him. "And Tucker was incapable of taking care of himself."

She'd chosen her son over her husband. The truth was between them, like a third walker in their party.

There'd been no aloofness in her baby boy. He'd been

all about love and hugs and cuddles. "I guess I needed more touching than just for sexual purposes," she said aloud. But she knew it was more than that. She'd been swamped with emotion and had needed to be able to express herself naturally, fully, without fear of judgment. Bray had always loved that she was a practical woman. He'd told her so many times.

But even practical women had feelings. A wealth of them. And expression of emotion was a natural need. A mandatory one if you were to remain healthy.

She truly didn't know how Braden did it, going through life without any ups and downs as he did. She'd never seen him cry after their son died. Even at Tucker's funeral he hadn't shed a single tear.

"I'd have held you without sex, Mal. It's just that every time I touch you I want you."

Want. Not *wanted.*

There they were, back in dangerous territory again. Made completely so by the fact that she was pretty certain that she wanted sex with him again, too. Just because of hormones. Otherwise she'd have wanted it two months ago, wouldn't she have?

Sex wouldn't solve anything. It would be great to be in his arms again, to lose herself to the magic of his touch, to feel his lips.

But when it was done, they'd still have their problems.

The one thing she knew, without a doubt, was that she couldn't go through losing him again. Their friendship might not survive another divorce.

Chapter Fourteen

He wanted to sleep with his ex-wife. Even more than he wanted to have sex with Anna. Walking beside her that Friday evening, he had to face the fact.

And to figure out if he could possibly be reading her correctly because he was definitely getting vibes that she wanted him, too. Like she had before Tucker.

"I need to know if you have a history of twins in your family."

"I don't know, but I can ask my mom. Why?"

The question made it out just as he stopped cold and stared at her.

The grin on her face and the glow in her eyes in the fading dusk were brighter than any streetlight would have been.

"You're having twins?"

"Yep." She nodded and kept grinning.

Braden grabbed her, hugged her, started to swing her around and caught himself. Putting her down abruptly, he said, "I'm sorry, but I'm so happy for you, Mal. That is, if you're okay with it."

"I'm great with it. A little worried," she said as she started walking, being kind enough to ignore the way he'd just grabbed her. "I have no idea how I'm going to handle two middle-of-the-night feedings every two hours, but I know I'll figure it out. I want to figure it out. It seems so perfect to me. Birthing best friends."

"They're going to fight."

"I'm sure of it. But from what I've read, a vast majority of twins are really close. I love it that my children will grow up with built-in playmates and confidantes."

She'd talked some about her years in foster care, about the kids who came and went. Some she'd missed horribly, others not as much.

And it occurred to him that Mallory wasn't used to having someone hang around forever. Had never had that. Even her foster mom had faded away when she'd started a new life with a new family.

Everything seemed to stop for him. Right there.

Was that why she'd pushed him away after Tucker came along? Or, rather, had given everything she had to their son? Because she'd never really expected Braden to be around forever?

But being a mother, biologically connected to Tucker, she'd finally felt that she'd found that forever person?

He had no idea if he was right or not. But the thought made sense. A lot of sense. It didn't change anything, other than to give him some understanding.

He still wasn't the man she needed. Wasn't ever going to be able to "sit in her tears," or whatever the counselor had said. He didn't have it in him. And he wasn't ever going to be able to make up to her the fact that he'd robbed her of her last minutes with her son.

Living with her anger afterward had convinced him of that one. It wasn't something he'd ever choose to repeat.

But…twins. She was having twins.

Braden was still chewing on the thought long after he'd left her at her car and returned to his condo for the night. He'd half thought about driving back to L.A., seeing if Anna was available for a drink. But he didn't really feel like entertaining or being entertained.

What he felt was empty.

Which told him he needed a good night's sleep in his own bed.

So he got one.

The world and its problems could wait until morning.

Mallory didn't see Braden before he left to head back to L.A. He called her, though, to let her know that twins did indeed run in his family. His paternal grandmother had been a twin. Having never known the father who'd run out on them, he hadn't known that.

She'd asked if his mother had made a huge deal out of him asking, but he'd had that covered, as of course he would have. He'd told her that he was having his DNA ancestry run and the question had come up. He'd said his mother tried to press him, but he'd made shutting down his family's drama an art form. One at which he excelled.

Braden checked in with Mallory a lot more often after that night. By text, if not a phone call.

At her eight-week checkup she heard two heartbeats very clearly and sent him a recording. And by sixteen weeks she was showing. Braden was still seeing Anna, but he hadn't slept with her yet. Why he'd felt the need to tell Mallory about that, she wasn't sure, but she reacted as she always did around him—with kindness and support.

Though how you supported your ex-husband on choosing the right time to sleep with his new girlfriend, she wasn't sure.

The whole thing was starting to drive her nuts. To the point of wondering if she should offer to sleep with him just so he wouldn't do it with Anna. The fact that she'd had the thought scared the hell out of her. But she had it more than once as May moved into June.

San Diego's weather didn't vacillate drastically, but it was a hotter-than-normal summer so far and Mallory had taken to wearing sundresses to work. Her employees and parents all knew she was expecting. In the newsletter she handed out to parents as they dropped off and collected their children, she'd written a note explaining that she'd made the choice to be a single mother and had opted for insemination. For the most part, she'd been met with congratulations and support. Any who hadn't understood seemed to have kept their comments to themselves. She certainly hadn't lost any business over the matter.

To the contrary, her waiting list for students was growing.

Which made her think more and more about expanding with a second site in L.A. Not that her San Diego requests would get use out of an L.A. facility, but if she could double her income, she'd be a fool not to. She was having double the babies she'd originally intended, which meant double the future financial need.

It would take extra time. She wasn't kidding herself about that. She wasn't going to be getting a lot of sleep in the foreseeable future. Nor would she have much time apart from work and babies, but she didn't want or need any, either. She loved her career and she needed a family. Those two things were her joy.

She was reminding herself of that fact as she ran out to her car the first Wednesday afternoon in August to retrieve from her trunk the month's decorations she'd made the night before. She wanted to get them up that evening so she could sleep in a little later in the morning and not have to come in early.

"Hey, I was just getting ready to call you!"

She jumped, hitting her head on the roof of the car as Braden's voice sounded behind her. She'd seen his car in the parking lot that morning, but it hadn't been there when she'd headed outside just before.

Turning, she saw him, still in his SUV, stopped in the aisle behind her, calling to her out of his window. He always let her know what city he was in. That night he was supposed to be back in L.A.

"What's up?" she called over her shoulder.

Instead of answering, he pulled around and parked, getting out and reaching to help as he saw her lifting things out of her car.

She wasn't ready to take them in. She was sorting through them, arranging, so when she got inside she could go directly to the room for which the decor was intended. She'd have done so before she loaded them into the car if she hadn't been so darn tired the night before.

Carrying two babies was vastly different than having just one growing inside her.

She turned as he approached and saw him staring. "You're huge!"

"Hardly," she chuckled.

"You barely showed at all last time when you were

four months." He stopped talking but kept looking and coming closer.

Before she realized what he was doing, he'd put his hand on her stomach. "Can you feel them yet?"

Their eyes met and though neither of them looked away, his hand dropped away.

He used to love feeling Tucker kick from inside her. She'd forgotten that until right then. The look on his face the first time he'd felt their son had been like he'd seen God face-to-face. He'd been so fascinated by that proof of the life growing in her and he'd wanted to know how it felt.

Was he remembering that now?

"I haven't felt them yet," she said. "But the doctor says it could be any time."

He nodded, looking uncomfortable, so she did what she knew to do.

Bring them back to his comfort zone. Business.

"I've reconsidered and I've decided to accept your offer to take The Bouncing Ball with you to L.A."

"Oh, good!" He grinned. "I'm glad to hear that. I'll have my contractor contact you with any questions he has when he gets to that part of the building. It's being framed now, but the basic building will be just like here, and electric will run the same as well, so your outlets will be in the same places. But if you'd like door placements changed or anything, you'll have a chance for input on that."

She cared about the fact that he'd instinctively wanted to feel her baby kick. Not about doors. She cared that his lips looked like she had to touch them with hers.

And while he talked about countertops and light fixtures, she wondered what he'd do if she quieted him with a kiss wet and hot.

Then he reached into her car for the entire pile of decorations, lifting them up and out, waiting for her to lock up before he followed her inside.

Braden was halfway back to L.A., looking forward to a quiet dinner with Anna, when Mallory called.

"You said you were just getting ready to call me, but never said what for."

He had, in fact, said that when he'd seen her in the parking lot earlier. But all too soon what he was about to say hadn't mattered as much as getting the hell out of there. He wasn't sure what it was about her these days, but every time he saw her he was out of sorts. Not himself.

She was having a baby without him. Kind of what she'd done the first time around, too.

"I was going to ask if you'd had any further thoughts about putting my name on the birth certificates. I know there's still plenty of time to decide, but if we're going to have legal things drawn up, we should probably start thinking about hiring someone to do that."

He'd just lied to her. That wasn't what he'd intended to call her about at all. He'd been going to tell her that he'd be back in town midweek if she'd like to schedule a meal together. And at the meal he'd have brought up the other topic.

"Now that there are two babies, it just seems more pertinent that we get this settled. You don't want to take any chances that they get split up."

He was pressuring her. He could see it, but it kept coming out.

"I'm just not sure it's fair to you," she said. "It leaves the door open for all kinds of things to get messy down the road."

"Not if we neatly and legally tie up all ends before-hand."

"What happens when one of them needs to see their birth certificate for something, like getting a marriage license or a driver's license or a passport, and sees your name? What if he or she decides they want to meet you?"

She was planning to tell her children that they'd been conceived by artificial insemination by a donor. How confusing would it be to have a father's name on the birth certificates?

"I was thinking about that, too," he said, tense and wanting a shot of whiskey. Since he was driving, he'd have to settle for ordering one at dinner.

That would amount to him having more whiskey in the last four months than he'd had in the last four years. This woman and her babies were driving him to drink.

"You were thinking about them wanting to meet you?" she prompted him.

"Thinking about them not knowing about me. Don't you think, if something ever happened to you, it would be better for them to have heard that I exist before they're suddenly faced with being uprooted and having to come live with me?"

"If they know about you they'll want to see you. This is why I didn't want to do this to begin with. It's already getting too complicated."

He'd talked her into it. Promised her it wouldn't be complicated. That he'd let her do her thing.

"You're right," he said, and meant it.

But he couldn't stop thinking about the fact that he was going to have two children in the world who might one day find out that he'd known about them and then think, by his lack of participation, that he hadn't wanted them.

True, he'd had no plans to have children, at least not then, and not with their mother. He'd donated his sperm for Mallory because she'd wanted a baby and his sperm gave her the security she wouldn't have had with an unknown donor.

His intentions had been good, but he couldn't have his own children thinking he didn't want them.

Except that he had no other choice.

He had to find a way to let this go.

The nights were the worst. She knew this. Clarity was less prevalent in the dark. When one slept, one let go of one's control of rational thought. And Mallory's uncontrolled, irrational thoughts were the stuff nightmares were made of.

She'd had more than she could count since she'd found out she was pregnant.

She'd been prepared for them, she'd thought.

But the night after she saw Braden, after his phone call, she had a doozy of a nightmare. The twins—they'd been a boy and a girl—had disowned her because she'd smothered them. At first the smothering had been emotional. She'd just been trying to be a good mother, but somehow she'd become needy and controlling, with no life but them. And then suddenly she was outside with flashers blinking around her house—rescue and police vehicles—and her babies were inside, smothered in their cribs. She'd been sobbing, looking at their window, knowing that she'd done it.

As soon as she woke up, trembling, sweaty, with her heart pounding fast and hard, she got out of bed and went to the kitchen to brew a cup of chamomile tea.

She grabbed her phone as she sat down at the table with her drink. This was a time to call Tamara. But her friend would be in bed with Flint. The call might wake up little Diamond Rose.

And she didn't really need Tamara. She knew what was going on. The fear didn't have her in its grip.

She was in her own grip.

Braden wanted to have a place in the lives of his children. She didn't know how she was so certain, but she knew.

She'd cut him out of Tucker's pregnancy and much of the five months of his life, too. Not purposely. Not knowingly. Not even wanting to. But she'd done it.

It hadn't been healthy for her or Braden, and had Tucker lived, it wouldn't have been healthy for him, either.

Most likely he'd have been the product of divorced parents, living in two households.

She didn't want that for any child. And certainly not hers. She'd always promised herself, if she ever had a child, she'd make certain that home was one place that didn't change and that didn't end. For as long as she lived, her child would always have a home to come to.

Somehow she'd failed to include Braden in that plan.

He'd failed her, too, in many ways, but this…this was on her.

Braden might not have planned to develop feelings for the babies she was carrying. And maybe saying he had feelings was going a bit far. But he felt a responsibility toward them. Felt accountable to them.

Legally she had every right to deny him access, even with the birth certificates. Even ethically she probably had the right, based on how his sperm had come to be involved.

But morally?

Could she deny her children the right to know their

father when the man was someone who would bless their lives? Someone who would always be there for them? Whether she met an untimely demise or not.

Certainly they were going to know Braden. It wasn't like the two of them were going to suddenly stop being friends.

Sipping tea, she shivered. Everything was such a mess.

As she'd known it would be.

And she'd agreed to use his sperm anyway.

Because in the long run, what had mattered was the security of her children. And two biological parents who'd want them were better than one.

Braden had been right about that.

Picking up her phone, she dialed him. He was keeping her up nights, so he could get up, too. It was only when she heard his sleepy hello that she wished she'd thought a little longer before making the call. Like maybe until he was back and they were having lunch?

She didn't want to give herself time to change her mind.

But now a thought struck her. "Are you alone?"

His pause told her he was not and she hung up.

Chapter Fifteen

Pulling the hotel coverlet with him, wrapping it around his boxers like it mattered if the world saw him in them, Braden went out into the living room of the suite and called Mallory right back. She wouldn't have called if it hadn't been an emergency.

His head pounding, he cursed the fact that he'd allowed Anna to talk him into drinking more than he knew he should. She'd met him at his hotel for dinner and then engaged him in a where-is-this-going conversation. That had led to the fact he'd just seen his ex-wife and had some things to work out with her first, at which time she'd started drinking more than she should, too.

"Mallory, pick up," he said when her machine answered, aware that Anna was probably awake in the bedroom behind him. "Please. It's not what you think. Call me." He ended the call.

It's not what you think? Like he was some cheating husband who'd just been caught?

He was divorced for Christ's sake. Had been for years. It wasn't like he hadn't had sex during that time.

But he hadn't had it with Anna that night. Or yet.

Back in the suit she'd worn from the office to his hotel, she came out of the bedroom, looking better than he felt.

"I'm sober enough to make it home," she said, going for her purse. "I'm really sorry to have passed out on you. That's just not my style."

He'd carried her from the couch to his bed, thinking she'd be closer to the bathroom if she got sick, and he'd be close enough to help her get there.

"It was a rough night," he conceded, speaking as much for himself as for her.

"So…is this it, then? I shouldn't sit around expecting a call from you?"

Watching her, he wanted to be able to give her what she wanted. Thought he'd be able to. As soon as he got the thing with Mallory under control.

And he told her so.

"So…call me," she said.

"I will."

He meant what he said, but didn't bother going to the door as she let herself out.

Embarrassed beyond anything she could ever have imagined, Mallory didn't answer any of Braden's calls over the next couple of days. She texted him to let him know that she and the babies were fine. And almost texted to cancel their lunch set up for the following Tuesday.

They'd been through much worse. Their friendship, which had taken three years to build, was the envy of many. She wasn't going to lose him now.

But the thought of him with another woman cut deeply. All she wanted to do was cry. In fact, she was afraid that she would do exactly that when she saw him, which was why she seriously considered canceling.

It was just because she was pregnant. She knew that. She'd been extra teary with Tucker, too, and figured, carrying two, maybe she'd be twice as bad this time around.

But how humiliating to be calling him to give him what he wanted and have another woman in bed with him.

Every time she thought about it she wanted to curl up in a corner and hide her head.

In one sense, her life was fuller than she'd ever thought it would be again. And in another, she'd never felt more alone.

She'd be a mother, but not a partner.

Her choice, she reminded herself. And knowing herself, she figured it was a good one.

So why did it hurt so much?

She was trying to tell herself it didn't when she entered the restaurant where she and Bray had agreed to meet. It was a different place—Mexican, which she loved—and a bit further from work. He'd had an appointment nearby and had thought it looked nice.

He'd been right. Inside, the decor was colorful and bright, and the people were friendly. She felt at home as, at her request, they walked her through the inside to a private patio off the back. Completely enclosed by trees and greenery, the area hosted eight or so tables, with umbrellas over them. In the middle of them, a tall rock fountain, with flowing water, gave a feeling of privacy and peace.

All but one of the tables was full, so she knew where

she was going. She'd barely settled in her seat before Braden was there, asking for two glasses of ice tea and then privacy until they motioned for service.

She'd never heard him be quite so forceful. He wasn't impolite, but his usual easygoing, friendly demeanor was definitely not present.

"I'm sorry I didn't return your calls," she said immediately, trying to ward off any undue tension between them before it got out of hand.

He leaned in toward her, his tie caught between the wrought-iron table and his chest. "I did not have sex with Anna."

Waving a hand as though she wasn't suddenly light-headed with relief, she said, "It's none of my business, Bray. You can sleep with whomever you like. You know that."

"The point is, I didn't."

He was serious, looking her right in the eye. For some reason this was important to him. "Okay."

As he sat back, their tea was delivered, as though their waiter had been watching and waiting for his cue.

When the man left, Braden leaned in again. "And I'm sorry for pressuring you on the other stuff. These are your children. We were very clear from the first about that. My participation was my own idea and—"

She almost held her tongue. Because she thought ultimately it might be the best way to preserve their friendship. But it wouldn't be best for their children. Or for either of them.

"I'm going to put your name on their birth certificates, Bray," she said. "That's why I was calling the other night. I'd just woken up with this horrible dream and—"

She stopped. She couldn't tell him her nightmare.

They seemed to be reaching some new understanding, a more honest understanding perhaps, but there were some things that didn't change.

Braden's abhorrence of drama and emotion of any kind being one of them.

Her obsession with having a biological relationship above all else being another.

"Anyway, you're right," she said. "It will be far better for the kids. And as long as you're willing to have them know about you, then they should know."

Everything about him seemed to change. He sat back. His expression settled. It was as though she could see the tension physically slide from his body.

And she knew, in spite of her apprehensions to the contrary, she'd made the right choice.

Life was good. His building was going up. All initial inspections had passed. Potential tenants were putting in applications and things with Mallory were finally resolved. She was going to bring The Bouncing Ball to L.A. Braden was satisfied that all was as it should be.

Driving back to L.A. that evening, he was looking forward to the future. Mallory was happier than he'd seen her in a long time. As the legal father of her children he'd have a solid place in her life and the right to take care of her or her children if the need arose.

He was free to pursue a more committed relationship with Anna. If she was still interested.

Yes. Things were working out according to plan.

Except...

They'd talked over lunch about having a legal custody agreement drawn up. He was taking charge of it, paying for the attorney, everything. She'd have full custody and he would be signing away any rights during her lifetime. The children were going to be added to his will. She was going to set up a trust for the children, leaving them all of her worldly goods, and stipulating him as legal guardian of them in the event that anything happened to her.

He would not contact the children outside of his friendship with Mallory. If they wanted to see him, separate and alone, he would make himself available to them pursuant to arrangements made through Mallory.

The one thing they hadn't thought of was his mother and sister. The children were going to have a grandmother and an aunt who would adore them.

Dote on them.

Biological family to love them.

He dialed Mallory through his steering wheel, activating Voice Command.

"I just thought of something," he said when she picked up. It wasn't six yet. She'd still be at the daycare, but would most likely be alone.

"What?"

"My mom and sister. As much as Mom drives me nuts, she also loves like the gush of the ocean."

The pause on the end of the line didn't seem good.

"Just think about it," he said. "A biological grandmother could be something you want for them. If you do, let me know. I'll take care of it."

"Bray?"

"Yeah?"

"When do we realize that this is getting too complicated?"

"It won't be complicated," he told her, refusing to get sucked into the mire. "We make the choices here. Or rather, you do. You're in complete control."

He'd do what she wanted, even if he disagreed.

"I'm signing away all rights, Mal. But you asked for my support, which means you get my opinion." They'd established that from the beginning.

"I know."

"The second you no longer want that, all you have to do is say so." It wouldn't be all bad if she did, he told himself as he made the offer. He'd be completely free of entanglement from the past.

"I want it."

"So, think about it?"

"Of course."

Good. Yeah, so, life was all good.

Morning sickness didn't happen. Not even as she moved toward her fifth month. But she was tired. Sometimes it was all she could do to get through the workday, make herself a sandwich when she got home and then plop down on the couch.

She'd ordered a second crib, exactly like the one she'd bought.

The girls at work were throwing a shower for her.

Tamara and Flint and Tamara's parents had already given her a year's worth of disposable diapers through an open credit account at a local box store.

Tamara had news of her own to share, as well. She and Flint were going to try to have a baby. Her doctor had said there was no reason that she couldn't try to carry to full term, as long as she was emotionally strong enough to handle it if she miscarried again. With Flint and Diamond Rose there, loving her, Tamara was ready to try.

It was enough to make one believe in happy endings.

Yet as each day passed, Mallory was less and less happy. She wasn't unhappy. She was deeply, deeply thrilled to be having her babies. Thankful beyond any measure.

She'd made the right choice to have them.

And yet, she lived on the verge of tears. Pregnancy hormones, she was sure. But that wasn't all of it. Maybe she was more apt to cry because of them, but the source of the tears was real.

She wept for Tucker. For the shortness of his sweet life.

Sometimes she cried out of stark fear. What would she do if she lost either of the two precious beings growing inside of her?

And she cried for Braden and her. She remembered his reaction that day at lunch, when she'd told him he could be on the birth certificates. She'd felt him so acutely. And she'd known. Just clearly, calmly known. Tamara had been right. She was still in love with him.

It didn't change anything. He wasn't good for her and she made him a tense mess, too. The sadness of that weighed heavily on her. She carried it with her every second of every day. And she worried that she was going to pass it on to her babies. "A mother's emotional state as she carries her children has an effect on the unborn children." She'd read that.

Promising herself she'd work at being calmer, for her babies' sakes, she focused on the paperwork on her desk. Till the phone rang.

It was her OB. The week after her four-month visit, the week after lunch with Braden, she'd been in the doctor's office for a standard blood test, one that could indicate that one or both of her babies had one of several possible genetic disorders, Down syndrome being one of them. And with a few words—"We got a positive"—her life imploded again.

Her first thought was that she'd done it. Something was wrong with her.

She listened while the doctor assured her that they weren't worried. They'd done another ultrasound during that visit as well and all measurements had been normal. The blood test in question came up with false positives more than any others, the OB assured her. But she'd need to have more in-depth blood work done as soon as possible.

Mallory had to leave work, she was sobbing so hard. She couldn't believe it. Just couldn't believe it.

In her car, she drove around the corner from the business complex and then stopped. She shouldn't drive in her condition but she had to get to the doctor's office. They had an opening at their on-site lab that afternoon and she'd taken it. She had to know.

Had to be able to do whatever was possible to help her babies if they were in trouble.

The thought drew her up. With a hand on her already swelling belly, she made them a promise that she would do whatever it took to give them the best life they could possibly have. This wasn't about her. It was about them.

The doctor had said she wasn't worried. And now it was Mallory's job to stay positive. To do all she could.

And she would.

But as she drove to the office she wished she wasn't doing it alone.

She needed Braden. Wanted so badly to call him.

But she didn't.

Chapter Sixteen

Sometime after midnight that night, Mallory sat in the old-fashioned wooden rocker with the brightly colored cushions, a teddy bear clutched to her, and looked at the identically adorned, empty cribs on either side of her.

She'd fallen asleep on the couch earlier and had finally made it to bed around ten. But by eleven, she'd been wide awake again, her mind spinning with facts. She knew a lot more than she'd known that afternoon, thanks to her internet research. While there were many genetic disorders that could have shown up on her test, the majority of the most severe had been ruled out. She could have heard that one or both of her babies wouldn't make it through the first year of life. She hadn't heard that.

There was still a slight chance she could. And a greater chance that either or both of the babies could have a chromosome disorder that would retard their development in any number of ways. She'd have the test results on Monday.

Along with sexes for both children. It had been an option on the blood test, finding that out. She'd checked that box, figuring she'd have something to look forward to hearing when the doctor's office called her back.

Until then, she'd worry. As she clutched the teddy bear, she reminded herself that there was every chance the first test had been a false positive. She reminded herself of the normal ultrasound. And she told herself she'd love her babies, whatever the test showed.

The physician's assistant had told her that afternoon that one of the reasons they wanted to check further immediately was because one of her choices, depending on the results, would be to terminate the pregnancy.

She'd shaken her head even while the woman had still been speaking. And she shook it again as she sat alone in the nursery. She couldn't even consider termination.

Just completely wrong for her.

Laying her head back against the chair, she rocked gently, hugging the bear, looking at the glow of the night-light on the ceiling. Tears came, dripped slowly down her cheeks. And they dried there.

Her mind slipped back in time to a similar night a month after Tucker had died. She'd been in his nursery, sitting in the glider rocker she'd used every single night of his life except the last one. Holding a stuffed penguin Julia, her coworker, had given him. Braden, who'd woken up and found her missing from their bed, had come looking for her. He'd tried to coax her back to bed.

When she wouldn't leave the nursery he'd started in again about calling someone to take everything away. He'd said she was making a shrine out of the nursery and that it was unhealthy. That she had to get a grip on herself.

She'd sat right there in that chair, clutching Tucker's penguin, and screamed at the top of her lungs, telling him he better not dare take away one thing of Tucker's. "Haven't you already taken enough?" she'd screamed, referring to the fact that Braden had taken away her chance to spend Tucker's last moments with him.

She'd never been so angry.

Now, sitting there in the new nursery, thinking back, she could feel the anger all over again.

She felt it anew as she considered his probable reaction to her current situation.

He hadn't been responsible for Tucker's death. Hadn't been in any way responsible for what had happened. Yet, she'd blamed him.

She hadn't been able to blame her son. And his death certainly hadn't been the nanny's fault. Mallory had blamed herself, of course. Not only for leaving, but for her body maybe not quite developing the portion of Tucker's brain that was in charge of breathing regulation.

But mostly, she'd blamed Braden. Because he'd taken her away. Because he hadn't allowed her to experience the pain that was eating her up inside.

He'd wanted her to be like him. To be able to move on. But she'd hardly been able to move at all.

Braden hadn't understood that, which had made her angrier.

She'd blamed him for an act of God.

The truth was clear now and, wide awake, she sat up straight, glancing around the room like there were people there, aware of what she'd done.

She saw her relationship with Braden as if in movie form. A movie of emotions. The way she'd slowly pulled away from him, starting when she'd found out she was pregnant. The relief and the exhilaration of knowing that she'd finally have a biological connection on earth. That she belonged to someone.

She saw, too, that maybe, just maybe, she'd never thought she and Braden would be married forever. People changed. Lives changed. And those you loved moved on.

Her mother had tried to keep her, till her life required differently. Her foster mother had been there, until she'd moved to Florida and found a new family. She was fine with both of those circumstances, didn't blame either woman.

Nor did she feel sorry for herself.

Now she realized that all along she'd expected Braden to do the same. To move on at some point, when their worlds no longer coincided.

So when Tucker came along, maybe she'd pushed Braden on his way.

Oh, not completely, and certainly not consciously. She'd never in a million years have done that. But the self-honesty which she'd had to learn to access to recover from Tucker's death told her that she couldn't keep ignoring the fact. She'd cut Braden out of her and Tucker's lives far more than she'd realized. She'd been living a future without him, while he'd been right there with them.

And when Tucker died, and Braden hadn't been able to handle her grief, she'd just kept right on pushing him away with her anger.

He'd been wrong. And so had she.

She'd spewed ugly words at him for things that weren't his fault. And yet, she'd been unable to let him go.

Because she'd still been in love with him.

Some things hadn't changed. Maybe some never would.

But some had to.

She had to quit needing Braden for things he couldn't possibly give her.

That's why she'd opted to have a child alone.

It was the only way that was going to work for them.

And so she sat alone in the night. She fought debilitating fear. She prayed. And, eventually, she went back to bed.

Braden had a great weekend. With everything falling into place he was able to play a round of golf, at which he had the chance to speak with the owner of several apartment complexes who was interested in having Braden Property Management take them on. Mallory would be glad to know that his L.A. presence was already being noticed.

She worried about such things.

He knew better.

But he was glad to know that she cared. The same way he was glad to know that he was going to be formally acknowledged as the biological father of her twins.

Throughout the weekend he thought of it often, at random times, and each time the thought gave him a lift.

He and Anna had a nice dinner-and-concert date on Saturday night, but things took a turn on Sunday. He got a call telling him a condominium complex that was a client of his in San Diego had sprung an underground leak, and more than a thousand people were without water.

The city was claiming the issue was the responsibility of the complex. Insurance said it was the city's issue.

First thing Monday morning it became Braden Property Management's issue. He had an agent in charge of the account working on it and reporting to him.

But the owner of the complex, Alex Mason, also owned five other properties in the San Diego area, all of which Braden's company managed. He thought it best to be on hand. Just in case.

He called Mallory to let her know he'd be in town, and when she didn't pick up, he tried the daycare number.

Julia answered.

"She's not here this morning," Mallory's second-in-command said. "She figured it was best if she waits at home, just in case. She doesn't want to alarm the children."

"Wait at home?" He was confused. Wait for what? And he'd tried her at home. She hadn't answered.

"For the call."

"What call?"

A quick intake of breath came over the line. "I assumed she'd told you. She usually tells you everything."

About The Bouncing Ball, sure. Just like he ran most of his big business decisions by her. But...

"Told me what?"

"You need to talk to her, Braden. If she didn't tell you...it's not my place... I'm not getting in the middle of it."

He could hear children's voices in the background, as though Julia was out in a playroom.

"No, that's good," he said. "It's just...well, I tried her cell and she didn't answer. Should I be concerned?"

"Try her again. Maybe she was on the phone."

Hanging up, he tried Mal's cell again. She picked up on the second ring.

"Hey, just calling to let you know I'm in town," he said. "I drove down early this morning." He told her about the water leak. She knew the account well. It had been his first big one. They'd celebrated the signing of that deal with a weekend in Cabo.

She asked a couple of questions about the situation, wanting to know why the city thought they weren't responsible for their own plumbing, if anyone knew yet what had caused the leak. And then she said, "Okay, well, keep me posted," in a tone of voice that sounded like she was ready to hang up.

"I don't see your car in the parking lot," he said, not wanting to hang Julia out to dry. The woman hadn't meant to clue him in to anything Mallory hadn't wanted him to know.

"I'm working from home this morning. Going over the finances."

That was it. Nothing more. She did like to do her financial rundowns at home, so she could be certain she wouldn't be interrupted. But usually she did them in the evenings. He'd never known her to miss work for it.

"You feel okay?"

"Yep."

"Any morning sickness?"

"Nope."

He tried to remember back when she was carrying Tucker and to figure out what could possibly be going on with this pregnancy that would "alarm the kids."

Nothing. He had nothing.

He didn't like it.

"You want to meet for a quick lunch?" he asked her.

"Can I get back to you on that? I'm expecting a call and I need to be able to talk freely when it comes in."

"Sure, okay. And everything's good with you?"

"I'm fine, Bray. Just preoccupied this morning. Lunch sounds nice. I'll let you know if something changes and I can't make it."

They agreed on a place and time and he hung up.

He was disgruntled for the rest of the morning.

Half an hour before she was due to meet Braden for lunch, Mallory was dressed, choosing a calf-length, loose, T-shirt tank dress she'd found at a flea market over the weekend. She was ready to go, but she still hadn't heard from the doctor's office.

She had looked at The Bouncing Ball's books. She just hadn't followed any one thought process long enough to do them any good. Finally acknowledging her lack of concentration, she'd taken a hot bath with a reality show playing in the background. Then she'd done her hair and makeup while listening to old sitcoms.

What she hadn't heard was the ringing of the phone. And she had to leave soon.

She really wanted to see Braden. At some point soon she was going to have to tell him some of the things she'd realized about herself. And she owed him an apology. But not that day.

Right then, all she wanted was to see his lazy smile, watch him consume his lunch like it was his last meal and hear about the Mason account.

She wanted things to be good between them, for the friendship that had seen them through the past three years to survive.

Five minutes before she needed to leave, she called the doctor's office, explaining her predicament.

"The results didn't come in this morning," the woman who answered the phone told her. "We generally don't get the afternoon delivery until after two, so you're safe. Enjoy your lunch."

Tearing up she thanked the woman. Then, taking a deep breath, she told herself to get a grip and hurried out the door.

Braden headed out for lunch ten minutes earlier than he might have if he hadn't spent the morning being visited by various scenarios of what could possibly be wrong with Mallory.

She'd said she was fine, but she hadn't said anything about the babies.

Surely, if something had happened to them, she wouldn't be fine.

No matter what it was, there'd be a way to handle it. There always was.

Still, he'd feel better knowing what it was he might be helping her handle.

If she'd needed his help, she'd have called.

And so it went. All morning long. Anytime he had a break in between calls.

Which, thankfully, hadn't been often.

He knew the second he saw her being seated at the table that something was up. She had a small furrow between her brows and her lips were tight. Until she saw him approaching. Then she smiled.

The light in her eyes gave him a lift.

"Bad morning?" he asked as he took his seat across from her at a little table for two by a column in the middle of the well-known sandwich shop.

She shook her head, but he didn't believe her.

She'd stayed home to go over the books. Was her problem financial? Had something happened with the business that she wasn't telling him about?

But how would a phone call regarding her financial situation upset the kids?

Maybe the problem was with one of the parents from her daycare?

A flashback to the year before reminded him of the couple who'd come into the daycare, claiming that one of Mallory's kids was the abducted son of a woman from Mission Viejo. She'd called Braden immediately and they'd met with the couple to discuss the situation.

Mallory had been noticeably upset by the whole thing, and seeing that could upset the kids.

So, yeah, maybe it was something with a parent.

She ordered tea from the waitress who approached. He did the same.

"I'm assuming, since you're here, your call came in?" Her business was her business, he reminded himself. She could share with him or not at her discretion. But not knowing what was going on wasn't sitting well with him.

Mallory shook her head. "I had confirmation that it will be sometime after two," she told him and looked at her menu.

She wasn't going to tell him.

So he let it go. He looked at his own menu, though suddenly he didn't give a damn what he ate.

"Mallory?"

She glanced over at him.

"Please, tell me what's going on. What's this call you're expecting?"

Her frown was full-scale, her hair jumbling around her shoulders as she shrugged and shook her head at the same time.

"Julia told me you stayed home to get it because it could upset the kids. She thought I knew what it was about. And she clammed up the second she realized I didn't."

"Oh." She watched him, seeming to consider something.

"Don't blame her. She's got your back completely."

"I know that. I'm sure she'll tell me about your call as soon as we next speak."

He was sure of it, too, which had been part of the reason he'd said what he had. But only partly. He mostly wanted her to tell him what was going on.

How did a guy fix something if he had no idea what to fix?

"It's nothing," she said now. "Nothing that you can do anything about."

He didn't know that. Not until he knew what it was.

"You know you don't have to take on every single one of my problems, Bray." Her smile was calm, almost serene.

That didn't set well with him, either.

"I know you can make it just fine on your own. I'm not trying to imply otherwise, even to myself. Or to think that I'm the save-the-day guy. I know full well I'm not. It's just…"

He needed her to understand. "I think about you," he told her. "I'd like to know that you're okay and—"

"I'm okay," she interrupted and he held up a hand.

"And to know that if something's bothering you, enough so that you stay home from work, and I'm right here and know something's going on, that— Oh for God's sake, Mal, please tell me what's going on."

She grinned, but it lasted only a second.

"I had a genetic defect positive come back on some blood work last week. The doctor isn't worried. It's not all that unheard of for this particular test to show false positives. I had a more in-depth test done on Thursday and I'm expecting the results today." She met his gaze the entire time she delivered the news.

And then she glanced at her menu as though there really was nothing big going on.

"You're telling me that the babies have something wrong with them?" And she hadn't called him immediately?

"Did you call Tamara?" he asked when she didn't answer.

"Yesterday," she said, turning the page of the menu. She was studying the thing like she couldn't make up her mind what she wanted.

He knew what she was going to order, so she must, too.

Reaching across the table he took her hand. She glanced over at him, a sheen in her gaze that was unmistakable.

Mallory wasn't as undisturbed as she seemed.

"You going to have the cranberry-and-turkey salad?" he asked.

She nodded.

He let go of her hand.

And they ate lunch.

Chapter Seventeen

The second he'd seen a hint of the emotion boiling up inside her, he'd shut down. Mallory recognized the response.

And so she did what their friendship required. She ate lunch. As much of it as she could get past the lump in her throat.

Her babies needed nourishment no matter what they were facing. Most particularly considering what they might be facing. They could have more than the normal challenges ahead of them.

Braden chatted about the Mason situation. The pipes in question became the responsibility of the owner when they were so many feet from the street. And an insurance policy, acquired by Mason before Braden Property Management was in the picture, required a rider to cover them. Braden had gotten a quote from a plumber to fix the problem. And he and Mason had decided to cover the cost.

They were also adding the underground plumbing rider to all of Mason's property policies.

She heard it all as she sat there, watching him. But she couldn't help the worry and fear from taking residence in her mind, as well.

On their way out to their cars, she finally explained the test to him. "It was a genetic disorder blood test. It looks for chromosomal abnormalities. That can be anything from a lack that often leads to death within the first year of life, or ones which could still provide a perfectly normal life expectancy. It could be trisomy 21, Down syndrome, which could be high functioning or not. There are others. A lot of them mean some level of developmental delay. If the babies are identical, it will most likely affect both of them. If they're fraternal, meaning they come from two eggs, it could go either way. The test seemed to indicate that it's not the most severe. And the doctor specifically stated that she wasn't particularly worried."

She smiled at him. "I've weathered worse, Bray. I'm going to be fine, no matter what we find out."

He didn't look convinced. He walked her to her car, waited while she let herself in and then shut the door behind her.

When he still stood there, she rolled the window down.

"Call me," he said. "When you hear, call me."

She nodded.

She'd have done so anyway.

He was her friend and she needed his support.

Braden was on his phone before he'd left the parking lot, arranging to stay in San Diego for the night. He'd had a dinner meeting that evening in L.A. that had to be rescheduled, and appointments in the morning, but he was able to fill his calendar in San Diego for the rest of the afternoon and set up a couple of video calls for the next morning.

He'd established a system that would allow him to work from either location, and it was serving him just fine.

He called Anna and let her know his business in San Diego was taking longer than he'd expected. She didn't ask if he'd be seeing his ex-wife while he was in town. He liked that about her. She didn't get all up in the drama of a situation.

He planned a sit-down with William, glad to have some time to spend with the man who kept his life running on time and on target.

In the meantime he was able to book a cancelled spot with the new physical trainer in the gym on the bottom floor of his building.

Up until his former trainer had been arrested—for having kidnapped his son—Braden had trained twice a week. He needed to get back with it.

The workout was good. He kicked it, hard, and came out sweating so much he stank. Showering off in his office suite, he changed back into his suit and looked at his phone. Three thirty and still no call from Mallory.

He'd had the cell on and with him in the gym. He'd even left it on the counter by the shower.

He couldn't plan his evening until he knew that Mallory wouldn't need him for anything. Not that there'd be much he could do. He wasn't a doctor. Or a miracle worker.

But he'd told her to call.

A knock sounded on his door.

"Come in," he barked, so not like him. He settled an apologetic smile on his face as the door swung inward.

Mallory stood there, a grin all over her face. She closed the door behind her.

"We're good," she said as she advanced. "Everything's fine."

Just when he was going to congratulate her he went weak for a second. He told himself it was because he'd pushed his muscles hard and probably needed a salty drink.

"They're fine?" he asked, standing in place so he didn't make an idiot of himself.

"Yep." She was right up to him, standing there, looking all expectant.

"What?"

"You want to know what we're having?"

What we're *having*, he repeated to himself, making note of the word choice.

"You know the sexes?"

"It was an option on the test," she told him.

"So?"

"Girls. We're having two girls. And they're pretty sure there's only one sac which means they're identical. They'll be able to tell that more clearly later, and it's still not for sure. They can do a DNA cheek swab after they're born to be absolutely certain."

Girls. Mallory was having two girls.

No boys who would need him.

It fit. It was right.

Pulling her to him, he held her tight.

Just so thankful that all was well.

She didn't mean to kiss him. There was no place in Mallory's plans for anything but the most platonic of friendships with Braden, but with her body pressed up against his, her breasts tingling from the contact with his chest, she didn't think about plans. She didn't think at all. Lifting up ever so slightly, she brought her lips closer to his. Watching them the space between his mouth and hers faded. The first touch was hello. The second… Mallory devoured the taste of Braden, the familiar touch of his tongue, the way his mouth said more to her in a kiss than it ever did with words.

She moaned, instantly needing more. Thinking about the quickest way to get her sweet spot free, about reaching for the zipper on his fly. Her entire being burned with that one touch of their lips. Bringing out the wild woman he found in her.

She didn't know who sprang back first, would like to think they'd both done so simultaneously.

"What was that?" she asked, out of breath, when he stood there looking almost pained.

"Yeah, I don't know," he tried for a chuckle.

Backing away, she moved toward the door. "I know you're busy." Half panting still, she was relieved one of them had stopped them before they'd made an irrevocable mistake. And was sad, too. "I just got a bit carried away there with the good news. Emotionally and all."

"Yeah," he said, standing right where she'd left him.

She was almost through the door when he called her back. "Mal?"

"Yeah?"

"I'm glad they're okay."

She nodded.

"And that they're girls."

She was, too. Boys would have been just as great, just as special. But Tucker was Tucker. For now, he was her boy. And she had two little girls coming who'd know his name from the very beginning. They'd grow up learning to love the big brother they'd never met.

They'd know their father, too.

From a distance.

With girls on the way, there was no way she could even think about more than friendship with Braden. If he thought handling Mallory's emotions was too much, she could just imagine what he'd be like with pubescent twin girls running around.

His frustration with emotional outbursts was one thing she'd protect her girls against. They were never going to be ashamed of who and what they were. Not as long as she was alive and in control.

And if she taught them right, they'd be fine even after she was gone.

Her lips were still tingling, her tongue still tasting Braden, long after she'd left his office. And that was something she'd have to get control over, too.

Immediately.

Praying it was just pregnancy hormones amping up her sex drive, she went to the daycare and put her mind to tasks that mattered.

Braden couldn't get her kiss off his mouth. He couldn't get the feel of her body out of his mind. He couldn't get rid of his hard-on long enough to think straight.

And he couldn't get enough of the salty drink to restore his electrolytes and get himself back on an even keel.

So he went to work. It's what he knew. What he did.

He put Mallory, her babies, their health and especially her kiss out of his mind and focused on making money. Lots of it.

For another hour he sat in his office and made calls, setting up more appointments for the next day. The morning in San Diego, the afternoon in L.A.

He had dinner at a pub with William, discussed accounts, members of his staff and the raise he'd offered the younger man.

He was putting William in charge of the San Diego office in his absence. The announcement would be made at the next staff meeting, but he didn't expect anyone to be surprised. The man might sit out front— his choice—but he was brilliant when it came to real estate.

Over a second beer, he asked William if he'd be willing to spend time in L.A., as well. William said he'd spend it in Alaska if it meant making money at a company that still put integrity and people at the top of the list.

And then dinner was over. William had a date waiting for him at the bar, a gentleman who'd been at the last holiday party. A boat builder, Braden thought, if he was remembering correctly.

It was a little after eight and he had nowhere to be. Nowhere to go but home. He could stay and drink more, but then he'd have to call a cab and wake up in the morning with the hassle of needing to get back to his car.

Paying the tab, he left, pulled off his tie as he walked to his SUV. He thought a drive down by the pier might clear his head.

He drove through the Gaslamp District and Balboa Park. He'd been in San Diego so long, he'd forgotten how the city had first drawn him.

When he passed by an entrance to the zoo, he thought about Mallory and her daughters. In his mind he saw the three of them laughing as she held their little hands and taught them something important about the animals.

Monkeys, he thought.

Mallory liked the monkeys best.

He ended up at her house. Maybe he'd known all along that was where he was headed. Maybe he'd just been giving himself time to change his mind. To come to his senses.

Senses didn't seem to matter anymore.

Mallory had spent an entire weekend alone, in fear for her daughters' lives. Alone. Just as she'd been most of her life.

It was criminal.

He knocked on the door, saw her peek out the side window a minute or so later and then, turning on the porch light, she opened the door.

"Can I come in?"

"Of course."

She was frowning as she opened the door wider and stepped aside.

She'd changed from the T-shirt dress to a pair of cotton shorts and a tank top. She wasn't wearing a bra.

When she caught him staring at the lusciousness taunting him, she crossed her arms over her chest and left the room, returning less than thirty seconds later wearing a baggy T-shirt.

"I wasn't expecting company," she said, crinkling her bare toes into the carpet.

"Marry me."

Her hands dropped to her sides. She half fell backward into the chair behind her. "What?"

"Marry me."

That was it. He didn't have anything else.

"Braden? Are you okay? What's wrong?" Her mouth hung open.

"I'm fine."

"Have you been drinking?"

"I had a couple of beers. You know I don't drive past my limit."

She nodded.

He liked that she knew him.

He waited, silent, until she spoke.

"I can't marry you, Braden," she finally said.

"Why not?"

"We'd hate each other within a year."

"Maybe not."

"Trust me, we would."

"We don't hate each other now."

"We aren't married now."

"You want me."

She licked her lips and he got hard. "Yes, but it could just be pregnancy hormones. And even if it isn't, that doesn't take away the fact that we're too different, Bray. I drive you nuts. You hurt me."

"I haven't hurt you lately." He hoped to God that was true. If he had, she hadn't said so.

"I'm not married to you."

She would listen to logic. It was one of the things he'd always loved about her. No matter how upset she might be, she listened to logic.

"It's the only thing that makes sense, Mal. Look at us. Three years divorced and we're right back where we started. A new building is going up, same plans, same daycare, and—" he stared at her stomach "—you're having my daughters."

He sat down on the corner of the couch closest to

her. He leaned over and took both of her hands in his. "We can't get away from each other, Mal."

"We were no good together."

"We were at first."

"Because we didn't have any real challenges to face. Everything was going our way. It was all fun and games."

He thought back and had to concede that she was right.

"But," she said, "when times got tough, when hard stuff happened—"

"—we made mistakes," he said, cutting her off before she could get into all that. No point in rehashing what they both knew.

She pulled her hands away from his.

"It was more than that, Bray. I realized recently that I never expected our marriage to last forever."

The words felt like a stab to the gut.

"Not because I didn't love you, but because I did. Love doesn't hang around forever in my world. At least I didn't think it would."

Adrenaline pumped through him. The salty pub food he'd had for dinner must have replenished his electrolytes.

"So at least I've proven that wrong," he said. "Even a divorce didn't keep me away."

Her stare had his heart thumping hard. Was she really going to consider his proposal? Did he want her to?

"I'm sorry that I didn't share Tucker's life and my first pregnancy with you more," she said. It wasn't quite what he'd been expecting her to say.

"It's in the past, Mal. Like I said, we both made mistakes."

"After he died I was so angry and had no one to take it out on. That, I shared all over you," she said.

Again, he thought he'd heard enough of the past. "It's okay, Mal. It's over." He took her hand again. "It's time to move on, just like we both said. And it's clear that we need to do it together."

She took her hand away. Braden watched her, trying to assess how she felt, trying to get them back to logic.

"It's not over, Bray." Her eyes had a suspicious sheen to them. No. No tears. Not when there was nothing to cry about.

"It's not over at all," she continued. "This afternoon is a perfect example of it not being over,"

"That's what I'm talking about," he said, energized again. "We can't keep our hands off each other. You know as well as I do that sooner or later it's going to happen. We're going to end up in bed together again. We can't stay away from each other, Mal. It's time to quit fighting it. We've got kids on the way."

The more he talked, the more she shook her head.

"That's not what I meant, Bray. I wasn't talking about the kiss."

"Then what?"

"Before that, at the restaurant. You wanted to be all in with what was going on until you saw that I was starting to cry. Then you were done."

He began to perspire. "Who says I was done?"

"You asked to order lunch."

And he had spent the rest of the meal talking business. He got it. He should have been more...

What?

The words of the counselor who'd done nothing but frustrate him came back to him. He should have "sat with her in her tears."

Or some such rot.

What did that really mean? Hand her a tissue? Sit and watch her cry for hours? Who did that?

He'd tried to console her during their marriage. Several times. Like that night he'd found her in the nursery, holding Tucker's penguin, sobbing her heart out. The nursery haunted her. Reminded her every minute of every day what she'd lost. They'd needed to get her out of there. To see that there was still good left in life. That there was more than what she'd lost.

But when he'd said so, she'd raged at him.

Standing, Braden shoved his hands in his pants pockets and strode to the window. He looked at the darkness and felt a storm building within him.

He took a deep breath, and another, waiting for calm to descend once again. He'd learned long ago that giving in to drama only made you do or say things that you'd either have to apologize for or that you'd feel embarrassed about. Like the time his mother had been running her mouth about Mallory, trying to convince him that she'd deliberately belittled her and his sister because his mother was jealous of another woman coming before her and his sister in his life. He'd lost patience with her. He couldn't remember what he'd said, but he remembered her response. "But, Braden, family always comes first and we're your family." What he remembered most of all was his response to that. "Not anymore we aren't." He hadn't meant the words. Not even the second in which he'd uttered them. And the pain they'd caused his mother, the doubt that still lingered from time to time that he'd cut her out of his life if she displeased him...

When he was calm, he turned around.

"We're having twins, Mal. Two daughters." He

should be there, helping with the responsibility. There'd be so much of it. At first, when she was still recovering from childbirth and both babies needed to be fed and changed and held, there would be two of them and only one of her.

They had to be practical. The rest would work itself out.

"And that's part of the reason this won't work."

When she spoke those words, he moved closer to her. She'd lost him on that one.

"Girls, Bray. Puberty. Drama. Think of your sister, multiply that by two, factor in me, and where would you be?" She was so calm, sounded so logical.

And then it hit him.

"You don't trust me with your children?"

"Of course I do. I trust you with their lives. I know without a doubt that you'll always be there for them. Anytime they call, you'll come running, no matter what."

Damn straight, he thought.

"But I can't have you around all the time, Bray. Not if we don't have to. The drama would make you nuts. And if you were here and then left, think how much more that would hurt them."

He turned back to the window, breathing deeply.

"Bray?"

He spun around. "What? What do you want from me?" He was yelling. Loud enough to be heard on the next block. Or so it seemed to him.

"I'm sorry," he said immediately. "That was uncalled for."

And then he saw the look on her face. Wide-eyed, Mallory stared at him.

"Don't look at me like that. I wasn't going to hurt you. I'd never do that."

"I'm not scared. I'm shocked, Bray. I think that's the first time I've ever heard you raise your voice to me."

"Yes, and I apologize. It's just…can't you see how frustrating this is? We belong together. It makes sense. I know you love me, Mal. I know it. I could feel it in your kiss today. And other times, too. Yet you're sitting here telling me that we can't be together for reasons that don't make sense."

"That's because you can't feel the results of them."

No, he couldn't. He didn't get it. But he knew that marrying Mallory again was the right thing to do. He sat down.

"So tell me how it feels."

"Your inability to understand my emotions makes me feel like a freak. It got so bad that by the time you moved out I felt like I had to cry in the bathroom with the fan on even when I was the only one home."

He stared at her. What on earth was she talking about?

"I was ashamed, Bray. Every single time pain welled up, I'd choke it back down. I hated that it was there, like it made me weak. And when I was happy or excited, you'd humor me."

He didn't remember it that way.

"You could never join me in being excited about anything," she continued. "Like this afternoon, I told you the babies are okay and you just stood there. I was ready to climb to the roof and fly, or to laugh and dance. But I'd have been doing it alone. When I told you we were having girls, again you just stood there.

"I got nothing, Bray. And that's fine for me now.

With us being friends. But think what living with that would do to our baby girls. They'd grow up learning to curtail their excitement, their joy and their sorrow, too, because little girls have an inborn instinct to please their daddies. You might not mean to teach them that, but they'd take it all in on an instinctive level. Just as I did."

Okay. Wow. Braden didn't have any idea what to make of that.

He stood. "So, just to be clear, you're telling me that because I don't get giddy or have crying fits, I'm not the right man for this family?"

It wasn't really what she'd said. But it seemed pretty damned close.

"I'm telling you that we're just too different, Bray, in a way that neither one of us can help."

So she thought he wasn't meant to ever have kids? Because he'd "rob them of their joy"?

That was another phrase from the counselor who'd done no good.

"I get excited," he told her. He reminded her of the time he'd caught a twenty-pound bass on a camping trip they'd taken early on in their marriage.

"Of course you do. But when the chips are down, when something is really important, bone-deep important, you aren't there."

"Where am I?"

"I don't know," she said. "Believe me, I've tried to figure that one out. You just space, Bray. And that's not wrong or bad. It's what works for you. It just doesn't work for me."

Sit in the fire with her.

Go deep into the woods with her.

He recalled the therapist's advice.

Mallory was right.

But it just wasn't him.

Turning his back on the only life that made sense to him, Braden quietly let himself out.

Chapter Eighteen

Mallory felt awful. On what should have been one of the best days of her life she felt like total and complete crap.

The only consolation, if she could call it that, was that Braden wouldn't be feeling the pain she'd caused him nearly as acutely as she did.

It killed her to hurt him.

To deny him.

She wanted him so badly, that killed her, too.

She was crying before he'd shut the door behind him. Great wracking sobs. She didn't even try to stop them. She just let them flow.

Five days of worry, of sometimes debilitating fear, of loneliness poured out of her.

What a cruel twist of fate that the love of her life would be a man who wasn't right for her. A man she wasn't right for.

It was worse than starting life with a prostitute mother. Much worse. Her mother had loved her enough to get her out of that life.

And while she'd never had a family of her own, she'd had a foster mother who'd loved her. Who'd kept her, helped her get to college.

She was healthy. Had a successful business she loved. Friends.

And now she was having healthy, identical-twin girls.

Still, she cried.

Because she couldn't imagine her life without Braden in it.

Sometime later she got up, took another bath, turned on the television and climbed into bed.

She'd survive.

She always did.

She had babies to provide for. Children of her own who were going to need everything she had to give. Children who didn't deserve a ripped-apart family and a torn-up mother. Which was exactly what would happen if she and Braden married and divorced again.

She couldn't do that to them.

Or to Braden or to herself, either.

As much as she hated it, she knew she'd finally grown up.

Braden left San Diego that night. He didn't make it all the way back to L.A. Instead, he found a hotel half an hour from the city and sat in the bar, watching a rerun of a baseball game and drinking beer.

The next morning, he was at his desk by six, sending texts to change the morning meetings in San Diego, making those he could video meets, and threw himself into each and every one.

He worked hard the rest of the week and into the next. It was what he did. What he knew.

When a decent amount of time had passed—meaning, enough for him to be right with himself—he called Mallory.

It had been almost two weeks since he'd seen her.

"I'll be in town tomorrow," he said. He had a meeting Wednesday morning with his staff and then a full day of appointments. "How about a quick lunch?"

He was going to tell her about William taking over the San Diego office for him, check in with how she was doing and then head back to L.A. that evening.

He might or might not tell her that he was no longer seeing Anna.

He'd broken it off with the woman when he'd returned from San Diego. He hadn't seen much point in continuing to see her. Clearly he wasn't into her enough if he'd practically begged his ex-wife to marry him while he'd been dating Anna.

"I don't think lunch is a good idea, Bray."

Mallory's response floored him. Almost literally. He dropped into his desk chair.

"What? Why not?" They always met for a meal, anytime either of them asked. That was their thing.

"Because we're just going to keep wanting more."

"But we're good, Mal. We know how to make it work. Forget the proposal. We're good."

"I can't forget it. I think about it all the time. And the kiss and so much else. It just hurts too much."

Wait. Just. A. Minute.

"I don't get it. We're fine. We're great. We have

plans. And just because I suggest we get married, now all of sudden it's over? All of it?"

It couldn't be. They were friends.

She was having his daughters.

He was going to be a father. From a distance, yes, but still there.

"For now anyway," she said. "I'm so sorry, Bray." She sniffed. He could tell she was crying.

"I'll call you tomorrow, when I get there. Let's talk then," he said and rang off.

He needed time to think. To find the logic. He knew, once he found it, it would save them. Ten minutes after they'd hung up, Braden texted Mallory.

You're not selling The Bouncing Ball, are you? Or moving it?

Her response was almost immediate.

No.

Okay, so they still had time. It wasn't over. It was just on sabbatical.

And you still want the space here?

He was pushing.

Yes, and fine, let's do lunch tomorrow. I can see we need to talk about things.

Damn straight they did. They were a team. Friends. Connected. They were having a pair of daughters before the year was out.

There was no way they could call it quits.

* * *

She just had to make it through one lunch. One more lunch as Braden's friend and then she'd be through with that part of her life.

It wasn't going to be easy. She knew that going in. It wasn't going to go well. She knew that, too. But they had history. They'd been friends a long time. She was a tenant of his and would continue to be one, and they needed to be good with that.

She was having his daughters.

That would be the hardest part.

But they'd done this. They'd made this mess. It was up to them to figure a way out of it.

When he texted, suggesting that he have lunch sent up to his office, her first reaction was to say absolutely not. The last time they'd been there together they'd kissed.

But the more she thought about it, she figured his choice was a good one. They'd need privacy to get through this meeting, for her to say what she needed to say. Chances were she was going to cry and she preferred not to do that in public.

After this, their dealings with each other were going to be limited to business.

A critical part of her life was ending. She'd never be in love again—not like she was with Braden—but neither could she be part of a mentally and emotionally unhealthy relationship.

He wouldn't be able to stand it, either. Not in the long run.

Just as he hadn't before.

She might have told Braden to get out when their marriage ended on their last bad fight. But he'd been the one to do it. He'd packed his bag, left and never spent another night under the roof they'd shared.

He'd come back to help her get the place ready to sell. To pack up his things. To take down the nursery and donate everything in it except the few things she'd already packed away, mementos of the son they'd lost.

But he'd never come home again.

She didn't bother changing out of her work clothes— maternity jeans and an oversize T-shirt—or dressing up, either, for her lunch with Braden. At twelve exactly, the time they'd agreed upon, she smiled at William and headed down the hall to knock on Braden's door.

She'd barely made a sound before the door swung inward.

Two Styrofoam containers sat on the table by the window, along with two glasses of tea. He motioned to one seat for her and took the other.

"You look great," he told her, glancing up and down her body as she approached. "I can't believe how big you are already."

She might have taken offense if she didn't know what he was talking about. "I know," she said, grinning. She hadn't gained anyplace but her breasts and belly, but she felt huge.

And she was loving it. Pregnancy, for all its physical downsides, really agreed with her.

He'd ordered her a grilled chicken salad with French bread on the side. She ate before she lost her appetite.

"So, have you thought of names yet?" he asked, digging into his container of spaghetti.

"Of course," she told him, glad that he was letting them start out nice and easy. Like old times. He was setting a tone that would, hopefully, get them through what was to come. "I was doing that before I knew what I was having."

She'd done the same with Tucker. Had chosen half a dozen names and narrowed those down to two before she'd thought to ask Braden's opinion.

He'd liked both of her choices and had left the final say up to her.

"Try them on me," he said.

She glanced up at him. He looked well. Fit. Too hot for her own good. She averted her eyes to her chicken salad.

"I went through the standards, Kaylee and Kylie, that kind of thing. But I really like Eva and Mari." She pronounced the latter with an "aw" sound.

He nodded as he chewed.

"Or there's Kelly and Cassandra."

He met her gaze and nodded again.

She went through a few more choices, adding middle names, as they ate. It was all very civil and kind.

"What do you think?" she finally asked when she was out of names.

"I like Madison and Morgan."

They hadn't been among her choices. She just plain hadn't thought of them.

"Madison and Morgan. Yeah. Madison and Morgan. I like them, too," she said, and they both smiled.

With that grin on her face, Mallory was gorgeous, choosing his names for their babies. He'd known to just back away, work, give things time to cool down, and everything would be fine.

It always was.

You just had to not get sucked up in the drama.

Like he had when he'd proposed. He'd been all up

inside himself, reacting instead of thinking. And he'd almost mucked it all up.

"Oh!" Mallory lurched, fork suspended, eyes wide. And then stark fear crossed her face.

"What?" He stared, tried to assess her expression.

"I just…" She shook her head and put a hand to her stomach.

"Is it the babies? What's going on, Mal?"

Her features had softened. "I think I just felt one of them move," she said, looking like some kind of madonna.

She jerked again, straightened, seemed to wait a second and said, "There. It just happened again."

"Is it the first time?"

He hadn't been present when she'd first felt Tucker move, so he didn't know if this was how it happened or how she'd reacted then.

"Yes," she said. "It's much stronger than I remember, from before," she said, half smiling. It was like she was there and yet not. She was probably tuned in to the children inside of her.

"Usually it starts more like gas bubbles, but this…" Her hand on her stomach, she stopped midsentence.

"You're sure it's not something wrong?" The sensations seemed to be coming somewhat regularly, and not minutes apart.

"I wasn't sure at first," she said, grinning now. "But it's definitely baby movement. It's not cramping, and it's not down low. It doesn't hurt at all. It just feels… odd. Different than with Tucker."

"Maybe because there's two of them in there sharing the same amount of space you had for one." Now that he knew for certain there was no danger, he was out of his chair, down on one knee beside hers.

He put his hand under hers on her stomach. Feeling Tucker move inside her had been the single most memorable part of the entire pregnancy for him.

He'd been moved—not drama-filled emotion, but different, calmer. More.

He felt nothing under his hand. "Is it still happening?" he asked, loving the feel of her roundness against his palm.

"Yeah." Her voice sounded different.

"I can't feel it."

"It's stronger than gas bubbles, but it's not that strong."

And there he was, his hand on her stomach, clearly hard. In his dress pants the reaction was obvious. She was staring at it, too. He looked at her when she raised her face, ready to apologize, and her eyes pooled with tears.

He held her gaze, reading far more than he could decipher in her look. She looked away first, out the window beside them. Down twelve floors or out to the horizon, he didn't know.

He cleared the table and threw away the trash.

She was right behind him with the glasses, taking them over to the bar where his cleaning service would take care of them.

She was the only woman he wanted in his life. She was having his children. He wanted to feel them kick inside her.

It was right that he should. Right that she shouldn't have to handle two babies alone.

He had logical reasons for their union. Their physical attraction was clearly mutual—and as hot it had ever been. But it wasn't just the sex. He wanted to hold her afterward, too. And before. To have the right to just walk into her home any time day or night. And to know it was his home, too...

"I came up here to tell you that I can't be friends with you anymore, Bray."

He turned, grinning. Thank God. She knew it, too. Had seen that them being married, not friends, was the only way for them to be happy. Somehow, this time they'd make it work.

She was standing at the sink, not doing anything, just standing there, her back to him. He moved toward her, wishing he had a ring to offer her. She'd kept hers from before. Would she want the same one?

She continued to speak. "If you're willing and in agreement, I'd like to continue our business association with The Bouncing Ball and Braden Property Management. And I will stand by my agreement to put your name on Morgan and Madison's birth certificates."

Something odd in her voice stopped him from touching her. He stood back, listening, thinking that this was her attempt to meet him on his ground, with logic, not drama.

It wasn't necessary. He could deflect the drama. He just couldn't sit in it with her. And that was good for both of them. She'd obviously realized that his control was an asset, that no matter how out of control things might feel, she'd always have him to maintain order in the chaos. To think while others reacted. To keep them from careening down a hill without breaks and crashing into little pieces.

He stood there while she continued.

"I will want the legal custodial agreement, with you signing over to me any rights to the girls, done before they're born. It's the only way I can put your name on the birth certificates. And that's all. Whether or not I tell them about you will be a decision made sometime in the future, as occasions warrant. I can tell you only that I would let you know before I said anything to either one of them. This is it, Bray. This is all I can do."

What? That last bit. What?

He stood frozen. Hearing her. Unable to process the ramifications.

She was over-reacting. That was it. Because of the sex. She'd said it would get the best of them, but couldn't she see that was a good thing? It was part of what kept bringing them back to each other.

"Take some time, think about it," he said. Time would bring rationality. Fear and panic would fade.

She turned, looked him right in the eye. "I don't need any more time. I'm not running scared here, Braden. This is something I know. We can't stay away from each other anymore when we're together. These babies have looped a new cord around us and it's drawing us closer every time we're together."

Exactly! So why didn't she see the obvious solution?

"When we're together, I need you to keep your distance," she told him. "Because I can't stay away from you. When we're in the same room, it's like you're a magnet, and I feel myself being pulled ever closer to you."

He took a step toward her, then another, his eyes intent on hers, silently telling her she was fighting the inevitable.

Holding up her hand, Mallory moved toward the door. "No, Braden." Her tone was unequivocal and he stopped instantly. "No more. Because when it gets down to everyday living and I'm me and you're you, it's not going to work."

She cut off his rebuttal. "Think about it. What if my test had come back positive a second time and I was dealing with possibly losing one or both of the babies I'm carrying? Or what if a few minutes ago what I felt hadn't been one of them moving? I know the risks I've taken on. I know I might face horrible heartache if anything happens to these babies. I know that I'm going to spend many nights watching them breathe, afraid that if I stop, so will they. But I'm also prepared to deal with that. And to deal, I may have to curl up in a corner and cry or sit in a rocker and hug a penguin. I can't do that when you're around."

She lay a hand on the doorknob as she continued. "And you...you need a home without drama, Bray. You deserve that. I love you and I know that's what you need, and knowing that I can't give it to you just about kills me, but not as badly as it would if we remarried and then divorced again." She shook her head, as if clearing it of the image. "I can't lose you a second time. Not like that."

It was logical. Every word of it. There was no drama. Just how he liked it.

With a nod, Braden walked to his desk, sat down at his computer and stared at a screen he couldn't really see. He heard the door open.

And close.

He didn't look up.

Chapter Nineteen

A week passed with no word from Braden. And then two. Mallory worked. She attended her baby shower, wept over the bounty of gifts and love her coworkers and friends showered on her. She had lunch with Tamara twice.

Her friend was pregnant. Tamara had never struggled to conceive. But with four pregnancies, she'd never been able to carry a live baby to term. She was having a hard time keeping herself above water emotionally as she faced going into her second month, and with Mallory grieving over the loss of Braden, the two of them made a sorry pair.

And yet they made it through each day. Not just functioning, but living. Hoping. Loving. Flint was a rock for Tamara, but it was Diamond Rose who was going to save her friend. The little girl who'd been conceived and born in prison was enough to show anyone that life didn't always work out as expected but it did work out.

Diamond Rose was still in her first year of life and already she'd healed two hearts and created miracles in two lives.

Mallory thought about Flint and Tamara and little Diamond Rose a lot. She talked to Morgan and Madison about them. They were a testament that she and the twins would know happiness. That things didn't have to be like a storybook to be right. That even when families weren't mom, dad and kids, they were still family.

Still candidates to be recipients for miracles.

It was that thinking that got her through the weeks without Braden.

At work, she watched the parking lot every day for his SUV. Once or twice a week she saw it there. Those days were better than others.

And harder, too.

When her phone rang on one of those days—Thursday of the third week since she'd severed their relationship— and she saw his number, she debated whether she should answer. The ringing stopped before she'd come up with an answer and then she debated whether to call him back.

Her phone signaled a voice mail before either side of her won.

"Mallory, I have the legal papers you requested. May I drop them off to you? Please advise."

She texted him rather than call him back.

I'll come get them.

She didn't want him in her space.

He was behaving like a sot. Someone he was ashamed to know. He could have left the papers with

William. Could have had his attorney mail them to her or to her attorney.

Perversity drove him to use the papers as an excuse to see her.

She'd get exactly what she wanted. He owed her that. But he wanted things, too. To see her. To reassure himself that she was getting along just fine without him.

And to clear up one other point.

If he was going to be free, he wanted it known that he was completely free.

She showed up at his office ten minutes after he called her. He'd purposely timed his call for her usual lunch break so he wasn't all that surprised.

In jeans and an oversize Bouncing Ball polo shirt, with a purple cardigan to match, she walked her matching purple tennis shoes into his office as though she had no idea she'd just poleaxed him with a shaft of pain so sharp he had to take a second to catch his breath.

Her hair was down, curled around her shoulders and lightly made-up face. And that belly. Already it was as big as he remembered her ever getting with his son. Which made him think about the back pain she'd suffered that last month with Tucker. She'd leaned her stomach against his back at night, using him to help her hold the weight of their baby. It had been the only way she could get comfortable enough to sleep.

She still had more than two months to go. How in the hell was she ever going to rest?

Not his problem, he reminded himself.

"You look good." He kept his tone neutral. No reason they couldn't be civil. Their differences were not the fault of either one of them.

"So do you."

He'd noticed her looking at him. For a second there,

hope flared, but he took hold of that response immediately. There'd be no inane reactions here that he'd have to pay for, or regret, later.

"Read this over. If everything meets with your approval, sign it in front of a notary and get it back to me. I'll countersign, my attorney will file it, and you'll get a final copy." He stopped short of suggesting that she have her own attorney look at it. Opinions and advice were a friendship thing.

She took the manila envelope. "Thank you."

He let her get to the door and then said, "Mallory."

She turned around. Relief flooded him.

He quickly put a clamp on it.

"There are some things that wouldn't go in the legal agreement, but that I need to have clear between us."

"Okay."

"Our friendship, the relationship we built these past three years, is ending. With that, all support ends. I need to know that you aren't going to call for advice or just to check in, that there will be no favors asked, or granted, on either side."

She blanched. He wasn't certain he'd ever actually seen someone do that before. His gut lurched but he pushed ahead.

"If, as you say, this has to end for the health of both of us, I find that I need to be free from all sense of obligation where you're concerned. When I go into a new relationship, I owe you nothing. My full loyalty will be to her."

He'd thought it all through, considering the reasons why things hadn't worked out with Anna.

"Of course." Her voice broke.

"I'll have my contractor call you when he's ready for

your input for The Bouncing Ball 2, as he's doing with every other tenant."

"Thank you."

He nodded. "I'm finished. You can go."

She left and he got back to work.

She was free. Completely, totally free. There'd be no more guilt. No more trying to be something she was not, to fit a mold that would make Braden happy.

No more worrying about him.

No more being concerned for his happiness.

There was someone out there for him. Someone who'd be concerned. Someone who'd actually make him happy—in good times and bad.

The good times were easy. It was the bad that had been their fatal trip up.

She read the papers he'd had drawn up. They were, explicitly, what she'd requested. The day after she'd seen him, she took the packet to her attorney for review. When she gave the go-ahead, Mallory signed them in front of a notary, with her attorney's receptionist as a witness.

She dropped them in the mail and told her babies they were going out for a treat. But after a few licks of a vanilla ice cream cone, she threw the rest away and went home. In the nursery, she sat in the new rocker, holding a teddy bear. She thought about the past and about the future, telling herself that while she felt ripped apart at the seams now, the future would be better.

Great things lay ahead for her. For her children. And for Braden, too. They just had to get through the dark moments.

She cried herself to sleep that night and woke up with tears on her cheeks.

Like she had after Tucker died.

And just like then, she told herself she'd get through this.

She was the daughter of a prostitute and a product of the foster care system. Her life experiences had given her strength.

The universe, fate, God—whoever—had blessed her with the ability to nurture. And so she would. Her children and others.

She would fulfill her destiny. Live up to her potential.

She would know joy again.

Because she was a survivor, wasn't she?

But, oh God, did living have to hurt so badly?

Braden spent the night in San Diego, mostly to prove to himself that there was no reason why he shouldn't.

The next day was Saturday and because he had no meetings, he decided to take the coastal roads back up to L.A. rather than joining the masses on the freeway.

Life stretched like an open road in front of him and he was going to find out where it led. He drove leisurely, stopping to have coffee and a muffin at a little café set atop a cliff overlooking the ocean. Later he lunched at a burger joint across the street from where he got gas. He thought about what he wanted to do when Braden Property Management was up and running in L.A.

Traveling sounded somewhat appealing. He and Mallory had always talked about vacationing on a Greek island, going to Italy and Paris.

He thought about calling his mother, to let her know that he and Mallory were no longer friends, but she knew all she needed to know when they'd divorced three years ago.

She didn't know about the twins. And now, all things going as planned, she wouldn't.

Cruising in and out of small towns, he took his time, watching people on the street, knowing that they lived differently from him.

And from everyone else, too.

When he realized the ridiculousness of his thoughts, he turned up his music and blasted tunes from high school, singing along when he knew the words.

Catching an outside glimpse of how ridiculous he was behaving he turned the volume down.

Mallory used to drive with the music turned up. She'd pull into the driveway of his apartment complex and he'd know it before he saw her car because he could hear her pop rock songs blaring.

He couldn't remember the last time she'd done that. At least when he was around.

Driving down a winding road, getting closer to the city, he slowed, not quite ready to arrive at his destination. The road narrowed as it turned sharply. Another car was coming and he had to get over toward the shoulder. His side had one, but the other side was blocked in by a rocky hill.

He took another hairpin turn, hugging the shoulder, and then it happened. He hit something.

Pulling off, he stopped his SUV, shaking as he looked in the rearview mirror. Something lay on the side of the road behind him. An animal. He couldn't tell what it was or if it was breathing.

Oh, God.

Getting closer, he could see that he'd hit a dog, some kind of smaller shepherd. He'd had an Australian shepherd growing up. They'd had to put it down when he was fourteen and his sister was eleven. She and his mom had carried on so much that Braden had been forced to be the one who carried the dog into the vet's office. And who'd dug the hole in the backyard to bury him. He'd had to act like it was no big deal or the two of them would never have stopped crying.

The animal on the road was still breathing but unconscious.

Scooping it up, he ran back to his SUV, laid it on the passenger seat and put the vehicle in gear.

It wasn't until he was back on the road that he realized he had tears on his cheeks.

Chapter Twenty

On Monday, a week after she signed Braden's custodial papers, Mallory was digging in her purse for Chap-Stick and came upon his key.

She'd forgotten she had it. Now she had to get it back to him.

Leaving it on her kitchen counter, she figured she'd put it in an envelope and mail it back to him.

But what if it got lost in the mail?

And how stupid was it to mail a key to the address it opened?

She didn't know his hotel room number. Wasn't even sure which of the properties owned by the chain he was at. They had two relatively close together near his L.A. property.

She could leave the key with William. That seemed the best choice.

Yet, what would he think, her leaving Braden's key? Braden hated company gossip of any kind, which was why, until the past few months, they'd rarely seen each other at work.

That's when she had her brainstorm. She'd take it to his condo, leave it there, locking the door behind her. She wouldn't be able to latch the dead bolt, but she knew the security code so she could reset the alarm.

Liking the plan, she put the key back in her purse and went to work.

The dog was still hanging on. Every day Braden had been making the half-hour trip from his hotel in L.A. to the veterinarian who had him. Dr. Laura Winslow was wonderful with the dog and with Braden, too. She let him come and go as he pleased, visiting the dog after hours when that was the only time Braden could make it there.

The animal had suffered a broken leg, which would heal, and damage to his liver, which might not. Laura had had to take him into surgery twice. They were now in wait-and-see mode.

Braden was footing the bill, of course, and in the meantime had put up flyers and asked all over the area to find the dog's owner.

There didn't appear to be one.

The dog was only about a year old, according to Laura. He'd had no collar, no identifying chip. He hadn't been fixed.

He could have been a stray or, more likely, according to her, a pup someone had left behind when they'd moved. It happened more often than people realized, she told him over coffee one night.

He was sorry to hear that.

Mostly he just wanted Lucky to get better.

That's what they were calling him. Laura needed a

name for her records so the dog became Lucky Harris. Braden hoped to God the creature was lucky.

Laura called him on Monday afternoon, eight days after he'd brought Lucky into her clinic.

"Any luck finding Lucky's owner?" she asked.

He was getting ready to go into a meeting downstairs in the conference room at his hotel. He'd arranged to use it as a temporary meeting site when the occasion arose. "Not yet," he said as he walked down the hall toward the elevator.

"Have you thought about what you're going to do with him if he recovers?"

He shrugged. He hadn't thought about it. "I keep thinking his owner is going to turn up," he said. "Let's get him better first."

He sure as hell couldn't keep a dog. He lived in a hotel suite.

"I think we're there." Her words stopped him on the thick carpet. "His liver is functioning at full capacity. He's up, eating. In my professional opinion he's out of the woods."

Holy hell. "You're serious?" The dog was going to live?

Her affirmative made him grin.

Mallory left The Bouncing Ball the second the last child was out the door on Monday. She'd been checking on and off all day. Braden's parking spot had been vacant for more than a week—and still was. Just to be sure, she called William, not to ask about Braden, which would be breaking protocol, but to make up some nonsense about needing the L.A. contractor's number, which Braden had already given her. She told William she couldn't get a hold of Braden, but not because she was no longer free to call him.

She and Braden hadn't set forth a rule to govern her business contact within Braden Property Management. Would it still be him, so that tongues didn't wag over the change, or would he pawn her off on William?

Either way, she'd abide by his choice.

"Yeah, he's in a meeting this afternoon," William said, his usual friendly self. "He's got more tenants than he can use for the L.A. facility and he's interviewing them all himself."

So he was in L.A. She had her confirmation.

William gave her the number she already had. She thanked him, rang off and turned her car in the direction of Braden's condo.

It took a second to find a spot in the visitor's parking section and another few seconds to wait for the elevator. Watching the security camera as she stood there, she felt like a criminal.

She was trespassing.

But she had to get rid of his key. She couldn't have any connection between them.

Ironically Madison chose that second to give her a kick, too close to her bladder for comfort. She'd named the lumps on either side of her. Madison was left. Morgan was right. For all she knew, they switched. And it wasn't like she'd know which one was which when they came out. But for now, the names worked.

Naming them had made her babies real.

She had two daughters.

She just hadn't been able to hold them in her arms yet.

Madison kicked again. And Mallory got the message.

The key she was dropping off was not the only connection between her and Braden Harris.

But it would be one less connection.

She took the elevator up and went straight to his door without a pause. It was like she had a demon at her back, pushing her to get inside his space.

It had only been a little over a week since she'd seen him. She'd gone a lot longer than that before, and she was now facing an entire lifetime without him.

Being in his condo meant nothing.

And yet it meant everything.

The second she unlocked the door she knew she'd made a mistake. The place carried a waft of his scent. Or so it seemed to her.

She remembered the last time she'd been there. She'd eaten lasagna off his plate. And she'd wanted so much more.

But that was back before she'd known for sure how messy it was going to get. How complicated.

How impossible.

Looking around, she started to tremble and then to cry.

Leaving his key on the kitchen counter, she quickly let herself out, locking the door behind her.

Lucky needed a place to sleep. And someone to watch over him, at least for another week or so. Braden couldn't possibly provide either. But he could pick the dog up from the veterinary hospital as instructed and watch over him for a night.

Which was why, Monday night, he found himself back on the road to San Diego with a dog curled up asleep in a kennel that was strapped into the seat next to him.

He couldn't take Lucky to the hotel, but he owned his condo, managed the property in which it resided and knew for certain that he allowed pets. Laura had given him some pads that she said Lucky was trained to go on, and instructed him to keep them by the door for Lucky to do his business for the first few days. Just until he acclimated to his independence a bit.

Braden had no intention of owning the dog for a few days. He'd keep him for one night and then he'd make some calls. Lucky was a great dog—a purebred, Laura thought. She'd have kept him herself if she hadn't already had two dogs at home.

People paid a lot of money for purebred shepherds. No doubt he'd be able to find someone who'd be happy to give him a loving home for free.

The condo felt off to him the second he unlocked the door. The dead bolt wasn't locked. Leaving Lucky's kennel just outside the door, he stepped inside to check the place out. Had he been robbed?

The security system was set, as he'd left it.

How had someone been inside without setting it off?

Two more steps in and he knew who'd been there. He could smell her perfume. She'd been using the same subtle spray every morning after her shower since before he'd ever met her.

Another couple of steps and his suspicion was confirmed. There, on the counter, was his key.

Mallory was getting ready to leave for work early Tuesday morning, telling herself and her daughters that it was the first day of the rest of their lives, when she heard a knock at the door. Who was there at six in the morning?

Frightened, she grabbed her cell phone, just as it started to ring.

Braden?

How could he possibly know she was in trouble?

"Bray?"

"Yeah, it's me outside. I should have called first. I'm sorry."

Rushing through the house in her stocking feet but otherwise dressed for work, she pulled open the front door. He'd sounded horrible.

He stood there with a kennel in his hand. She could see a dog inside. It didn't appear to be moving.

Braden's eyes were red-rimmed. His hair was a mess, his pants and dress shirt wrinkled.

Had he been up all night?

"Braden, what's going on?" She looked at the kennel again.

He didn't do dogs. Years ago she'd suggested they get one, thinking it would be a friend to Tucker growing up, but he'd categorically refused.

"I hit him," he said, holding up the kennel. "On the way back to L.A. last week, I ran over him with my car."

And he'd kept him in a kennel?

Opening the door wider, she let the man in. He was clearly not himself. She just had to figure out what she was dealing with so she'd know whom to call.

It briefly occurred to her that they'd just promised they wouldn't do this. They wouldn't call on each other in need or support each other.

But there was no way she was turning him away this morning.

He sat on her couch, putting the kennel with the unmoving animal at his feet.

"Have you been drinking? Are you sick?" She sat on the edge of the couch, a foot away from him. Should she call a doctor?

"No."

"You look awful, Bray."

"I've been up all night."

"I thought you said the accident was a week ago."

"It was," he said. "Nine days, actually."

The night after they'd last seen each other. She knew the number of days, too.

He looked at her. His chin trembled, his eyes welled. Tears didn't fall. At least his didn't.

Mallory's did.

"Bray?"

"It's not your emotion I can't handle, Mal. It's my own. I wasn't blocking you, I was blocking me. Seeing you upset would upset me, and so I blocked."

His shoulders were fallen, his features ashen.

"I'm a fraud," he said. "I lost my dad. And then Gonzo. I was only fourteen and I had to dig his grave. And my mom and sister... Mom could hardly cope after Dad left. And my sister, she blamed herself. I had to be strong."

Heart pounding, she sniffled. She put her hand on top of his and glanced at the kennel, too. They needed to call someone about the dog.

And maybe about Braden, too.

Had he really been living with a dead dog in a kennel for over a week?

Shouldn't it smell?

She squeezed his hand, more in love than she'd ever been. When they'd first been married she'd known that Braden had depths people couldn't see. She'd just *known*.

When had she forgotten that?

"I pushed you away," he told her. "I couldn't handle the pain of losing Tucker. Or the blame. I shut down on myself. And then you. I couldn't handle it. I'm weak and a fool, Mallory, and I'm so sorry."

"You are not weak. You're one of the strongest men I've ever known," she told him. "And you most definitely aren't a fool." She felt the truth of the words to her core. But still she worried.

Clearly Braden had had an extremely difficult eye-opening experience. But at what cost?

She hadn't ever meant to break him. Didn't want to break him.

"Bray, it's okay. I never should have made the ridiculous mandate that we can't be friends. Clearly we can't *not* be friends." She was crying softly but was able to instill all the certainty she felt in the words.

He shook his head.

"Where have you been all night?" He said he'd been up. Surely not driving around with the kennel.

"At home. At my condo."

"You've been here, in San Diego?"

"I had to have a place to take Lucky."

"Lucky." The dog, obviously. He'd named a dead dog?

"He got out of the hospital yesterday afternoon and needs around-the-clock care for the first couple of days. Knowing that he could die if I went to sleep, I didn't."

And the dog had died anyway?

She glanced down, afraid of what another loss on his shoulders had done to Braden's psyche.

And that was when she saw two big brown eyes peering up at her.

"Bray! He's not dead! Look!" She jumped up so fast it startled the animal, which moved suddenly and then whimpered.

"Of course he's not dead," Braden said, opening the

door immediately, reaching in first to pet the dog, talking soothingly, and then carefully lifting him out.

He had a cast on one of his back legs. And a bandage wrapped around his torso where the fur had obviously been shaved.

"I told you, I've been up all night caring for him," he reminded her. "Which left me far too much time with nothing to do but sit alone with myself." Holding the dog, he looked over at her and met her gaze fully. "I was scared to death he was going to die on me. Really scared. I couldn't leave him there, go to work, go anywhere. I had no one to call. It was all on me. And it struck me how you'd felt in the nursery that night I came in there and found you holding Tucker's penguin."

She was crying again, slow tears dripping down her cheeks.

"Helpless, that's how it feels," he said. "And sometimes there's not a damn thing you can do about it."

"Except sit with it until it passes. Trusting that it will pass."

"Sit with it," he said, his eyes opening wider. "Sit with it. That's right. Sometimes, loving someone means being able to sit in depths of despair with them."

She coughed, trying to hold back a sob, and failed.

"That finally makes sense to me," Braden said.

She didn't get the significance of the statement, but clearly it meant something to him.

"I'm so sorry, Mal." He pet the dog, but his gaze was on hers. "I let you down at the most devastating time in our lives."

"Shh." She put a finger to his lips. "I let you down, too," she said. "Even before that. If I hadn't, maybe you wouldn't have. Maybe you would've. But what matters is that for the four years since, we've been hanging on to each other. We've been trying. Together."

Even after they'd said they wouldn't be friends she hadn't been able to let go. Not with The Bouncing Ball. Not with his name on his daughters' birth certificates.

"It was your key on the counter that did it," he said. "You rescued me, Mal."

"It sounds like I deserted you alone on a night of sheer hell."

"Nothing that could even come close to comparing to my emotional absence after our son died. I can't promise that I won't check out again at some point, for a time, but I can promise that I will always come back to you, Mal. That I will sit with you, and our daughters, no matter what you're feeling. Please, Mal, say you'll marry me. Please." His eyes got moist and as uncomfortable as that might have made him, he didn't seem to fight it.

"Oh, God, Bray, I…" she started to cry, but was smiling, too. "You feel like a trip to Vegas this weekend? I thought… Anyway," she threw her arms around his neck, careful of her belly and the dog. "Yes, of course I'll marry you," she said, kissing him with all of the need inside her.

It was a few minutes before either of them could speak. Braden kissed her so hard they fell back against the couch. When she'd been ready to take things to the bedroom, he pulled back.

"And Lucky? You're okay with keeping him?" She couldn't believe it, but for a second there she'd actually forgotten about the dog.

"I wouldn't have it any other way," she said, petting the animal who was sitting there like he belonged to them. Looking at them like they belonged to him.

"I was thinking maybe I'd have William run the office in L.A. instead of San Diego."

She grinned through her tears. Leave it to Braden to have the logistics all worked out. God, how she loved the man.

"And that I'd like to take you up on your offer and drive over to Nevada today and get married. I'd say fly, but we've got Lucky."

"Driving is good," she said. He hadn't mentioned any appointments he might have that day, but as for herself, she'd call Julia and let her know she wouldn't be in.

Braden continued to sit there, petting the dog.

"Bray?"

"Hmm?"

"You can put the dog down and make love to me now."

He froze, then stared at her.

"It's just dawning on me how much it's going to kill me if I ever lose you again."

"It's not going to happen if I can help it, but even if it did someday, you'll survive, Bray. Because that's what love does. It gives you the strength to survive. No matter what."

She had to hand it to him. He had the wherewithal to set the dog gently on a blanket on the floor before he grabbed Mallory up, laid her down on the couch and proceeded to get emotional all over her.

And in her.

Because just like she'd told her daughters, as long as they existed, they were candidates to be recipients of a miracle.

They just had to be patient until it arrived.

* * * * *

*Don't miss previous books in the
Daycare Chronicles:*

Her Lost and Found Baby
An Unexpected Christmas Baby

*Available now from
Harlequin Special Edition!*

*And look out for Tara's next book,
coming June 2019.*

#2683 GUARDING HIS FORTUNE
The Fortunes of Texas: The Lost Fortunes • by Stella Bagwell
Savannah Fortune is off-limits, and bodyguard Chaz Mendoza knows it. The grad student he's been hired to look after is smart, opinionated—and rich. What would she want with a regular guy like Chaz? Her family has made it clear he has no permanent place in her world. But Chaz refuses to settle for anything less...

#2684 THE LAWMAN'S ROMANCE LESSON
Forever, Texas • by Marie Ferrarella
When Shania Stewart tells Deputy Daniel Tallchief that he needs to lighten up with his wild younger sister, the handsome lawman doesn't know whether to ignore her or kiss her. But Shania knows. It's going to take a carefully crafted lesson plan to tutor this cowboy in love.

#2685 TO KEEP HER BABY
The Wyoming Multiples • by Melissa Senate
After Ginger O'Leary learns she's pregnant, it's time for a whole new Ginger. James Gallagher is happy to help, but after years of raising his siblings, becoming attached isn't in the plan. But neither is the way his heart soars every time he and Ginger match wits. What will it take for these two opposites to realize that they're made for each other?

#2686 AN UNEXPECTED PARTNERSHIP
by Teresa Southwick
Leo Wallace had been duped—hard—once before, so he refuses to take Tess's word when she says she's pregnant. Now she wants Leo's help to save her family business, too. Leo agrees to be the partner Tess needs. But it's going to take a paternity test to make him believe this baby is his. He just can't trust his heart again...no matter what it's saying.

#2687 THE NANNY CLAUSE
Furever Yours • by Karen Rose Smith
When Daniel Sutton's daughters rescue an abandoned calico, the hardworking attorney doesn't expect to be sharing his home with a litter of newborns! And animal shelter volunteer Emma Alvarez is transforming the lives of Daniel and his three girls. The first-time nanny is a natural with kids and pets. Will that extend to a single father ready to trust in love again?

#2688 HIS BABY BARGAIN
Texas Legends: The McCabes • by Cathy Gillen Thacker
Ex-soldier turned rancher Matt McCabe wants to help his recently widowed friend and veterinarian, Sara Anderson. She wants him to join her in training service dogs for veterans—oddly, he volunteers to take care of her adorable eight-month-old son, Charley, instead. This "favor" feels more like family every day...though their troubled pasts threaten a happy future.

Shania flushed as she raised her eyes toward Daniel. "I don't usually babble like this."

Daniel found the pink hue that had suddenly risen to her cheeks rather sweet. The next second, he realized that he was staring. Daniel forced himself to look away. "I hadn't noticed."

"Yes, you had," Shania contradicted. "But I think that it's very nice of you to pretend that you hadn't." When she heard Daniel laugh softly to himself, she asked him, "What's so funny?" before she could think to stop herself.

"I'm not accustomed to hearing the word *nice* used to describe me," he admitted.

Didn't the man have any close friends? Someone to bolster him up when he was down on himself? "You're kidding."

The lopsided smile answered her before he did. "Something else I'm not known for."

She pretended that he was a student and she did a quick assessment of the man before her. "You know you're being very hard on yourself."

"Not hard," he contradicted. "Just honest."

She had no intention of letting this slide. If he had been one of her students, she would have done what she could to raise his spirits—or maybe it was his self-esteem that needed help.

"Well, I think you're nice—and you do have a sense of humor."

"If you say so," Daniel replied, not about to dispute the matter. He had a feeling that arguing with Shania would be pointless. "But just so you know, I'm not about to chuck my career and become a stand-up comedian."

She grinned at his words. "See, I told you that you had a sense of humor," she declared happily.

Don't miss
The Lawman's Romance Lesson *by Marie Ferrarella,*
available April 2019 wherever
Harlequin® Special Edition books and ebooks are sold.

www.Harlequin.com

Looking for more satisfying love stories
with community and family at their core?

Check out **Harlequin® Special Edition**
and **Love Inspired®** books!

New books available every month!

CONNECT WITH US AT:

Facebook.com/groups/HarlequinConnection

Facebook.com/HarlequinBooks

Twitter.com/HarlequinBooks

Instagram.com/HarlequinBooks

Pinterest.com/HarlequinBooks

ReaderService.com

**ROMANCE WHEN
YOU NEED IT**

HFGENRE2018

*Read on for a sneak peek at
the first heartwarming book in Lee Tobin McClain's
Safe Haven series,* Low Country Hero!

They'd both just turned back to their work when a familiar loud, croaking sound cut the silence.

The twins shrieked and ran from where they'd been playing into the little cabin's yard and slammed into Anna, their faces frightened.

"What was that?" Anna sounded alarmed, too, kneeling to hold and comfort both girls.

"Nothing to be afraid of," Sean said, trying to hold back laughter. "It's just egrets. Type of water bird." He located the source of the sound, then went over to the trio, knelt beside them, and pointed through the trees and growth.

When the girls saw the stately white birds, they gasped.

"They're so pretty!" Anna said.

"Pretty?" Sean chuckled. "Nobody from around here would get excited about an egret, nor think it's especially pretty." But as he watched another one land beside the first, white wings spread wide as it skidded into the shallow water, he realized that there was beauty there. He just hadn't noticed it before.

That was what kids did for you: made you see the world through their fresh, innocent eyes. A fist of longing clutched inside his chest.

The twins were tugging at Anna's shirt now, trying to get her to take them over toward the birds. "You may go look as long as you can see me," she said, "but take careful steps by the water." She took the bolder twin's face in her hands. "The water's not deep, but I still don't want you to wade in. Do you understand?"

Both little girls nodded vigorously.

They ran off and she watched for a few seconds, then turned back to her work with a barely audible sigh.

"Go take a look with them," he urged her. "It's not every day kids see an egret for the first time."

"You're sure?"

"Go on." He watched her run like a kid over to her girls. And then he couldn't resist walking a few steps closer and watching them, shielded by the trees and brush.

The twins were so excited that they weren't remembering to be quiet. "It caught a *fish*!" the one was crowing, pointing at the bird, which, indeed, held a squirming fish in its mouth.

"That one's neck is like an S!" The quieter twin squatted down, rapt.

Anna eased down onto the sandy beach, obviously unworried about her or the girls getting wet or dirty, laughing and talking to them and sharing their excitement.

The sight of it gave him a melancholy twinge. His own mom had been a nature lover. She'd taken him and his brothers fishing, visited a nature reserve a few times, back in Alabama where they'd lived before coming here.

Oh, if things were different, he'd run with this, see where it led…

Don't miss
Lee Tobin McClain's Low Country Hero,
available March 2019 from HQN Books!

www.Harlequin.com

Love Harlequin romance?

DISCOVER.

Be the first to find out about promotions, news and exclusive content!

f Facebook.com/HarlequinBooks

y Twitter.com/HarlequinBooks

O Instagram.com/HarlequinBooks

P Pinterest.com/HarlequinBooks

ReaderService.com

EXPLORE.

Sign up for the Harlequin e-newsletter and download a free book from any series at **TryHarlequin.com.**

CONNECT.

Join our Harlequin community to share your thoughts and connect with other romance readers!
Facebook.com/groups/HarlequinConnection

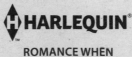

HARLEQUIN®

ROMANCE WHEN YOU NEED IT

HSOCIAL2018